Y0-CBH-205

LOOKING
Through Water

LOOKING
Through Water

A NOVEL

Bob Rich

Skyhorse Publishing

This book is a work of fiction. References to real people, events, establishments, organizations, or locales are intended only to provide a sense of accuracy and authenticity. All other characters, and all incidents and dialogue, are from the author's imagination and are used fictitiously.

Skyhorse Publishing books may be purchased in bulk at special discounts for sales promotion, corporate gifts, fund-raising, or educational purposes. Special editions can also be created to specifications. For details, contact the Special Sales Department, Skyhorse Publishing, 307 West 36th Street, 11th Floor, New York, NY 10018 or info@skyhorsepublishing.com.

Visit our website at www.skyhorsepublishing.com.

10 9 8 7 6 5 4 3 2 1

Library of Congress Cataloging-in-Publication Data is available on file.

Cover design by Brian Peterson
Cover image by John Swan

Print ISBN: 978-1-5107-0314-8
Ebook ISBN: 978-1-5107-0315-5

Printed in the United States of America

For Yesterday is Already a Dream and Tomorrow is
Only a Vision, But Today, Well Lived, Makes Every
Yesterday a Dream of Happiness and Every Tomorrow a
Vision of Hope.

—Ancient Sanskrit Poem

Contents

For my grandfather from the British Isles, who loved being on deep water, and my eight grandchildren, each of whom let me join them when they caught their first fish. And for everyone who has gained self-awareness by looking through water.

DEAR READER

I am not a writer. I am a storyteller, who, by definition, hates long introductions a lot and long books more.

• • •

A loving and thoughtful grandparent can change a child's life. If you have been blessed to have a grandchild, you have an obligation to become such a grandparent. This story is about just such a person.

Within these pages, a grandson becomes a grandfather and reaches back into his past to share with his troubled grandson the events of a week that would forever change his life.

William McKay was neither a sinner nor a saint, just a man trying to make sense of his life. He never set out to be a teacher but was thrust into the role, during which time he taught and learned as well.

Looking Through Water is not solely a tale of adventure, a love story, or a chronicle of one man's journey to self-awareness. It combines all of these elements to explore the dynamics of intergenerational family relationships.

While a quick read, I hope this story will entertain and instruct and, for many, bring back long-forgotten memories of the bittersweet journey of coming-of-age.

CHAPTER 1

LOCH LOON—2012

William McKay stood on the wooden dock by the fog-shrouded lake, listening to the plaintive cry of a loon as it pierced the morning silence. He cherished that sound, heard so often here from the time he was a young boy. Now approaching his seventy-third birthday, he retained the look of a former athlete, tall and slender, well tanned, with a full head of hair, now turned white. A three-inch diagonal scar on the left side of his forehead added an air of mystery to his handsome, chiseled face.

As the morning fog lifted, he scanned the lake with bright eyes and his ever-youthful curiosity, then climbed into the small dinghy and pushed off from the dock with ease. He felt fortunate not to wrestle with balance like so many of his contemporaries. He began to row across the mile-wide lake as he had many times for more than sixty years—since he was a boy. Now that young boy had become the old man. So much had happened between then and now; he wished he could write that boy a letter telling him what to watch out for, but he knew that wasn't the way things worked.

The lake had for many years been known as Iroquois Lake, named after one of the many Native American tribes that had inhabited the region. Iroquois was one of those Adirondack lakes that people referred to as bottomless. Early settlers in the region had dropped 150 feet of coiled rope from a boat in the center and not hit bottom. Its dark water, usually calm and always cold, held an aura of mystery along with an abundance of fish.

In the early 1900s, William's grandfather, a banker named Angus McKay, had moved his family to New York City from Perth, Scotland, where he had gained a reputation as an accomplished investor with a penchant for gambling. He won the lake and surrounding land from another banker in a game of poker. Angus's first order of business was to rename the lake . . . Loch Loon. Then he built a lodge at one end, setting up the entire property as a not-for-profit club and selling six pieces to Scottish American pals of his to build summer homes. He kept the choicest two lots, one on either side of the lake, for himself and, eventually, for his son. The transaction, like many of his others, gained him a handsome return and added to his reputation on Wall Street as a brilliant and daring entrepreneur.

Some years later, Angus left the bank and founded a small brokerage firm, which he named McKay and Son in the hope that his son, Leod—William's father—would come to work with him, and eventually he did.

Angus was defined by his business, working long hours—six . . . sometimes seven . . . days a week. He was in that office so often that many of his protégés swore they never saw him enter the building in the morning or leave at night. Angus simply outworked his peers, while along the way developing an uncanny ability to recognize great investment opportunities. Some looked at it as a gift. Others said he was merely lucky. Angus just smiled, knowing that the harder he worked, the luckier he got. At any rate, his good stewardship of money made him a sought-after manager by many wealthy investors.

If Angus did have an indulgence, it was Loch Loon. When his son Leod's school year ended, he would see the boy and his mother off at Grand Central Station on a train bound for the Adirondacks, where they would stay at the lake until the Tuesday after Labor Day. He would join them for two solid weeks beginning with the Fourth of July and for as many weekends as he felt he could get away from Wall Street. His time at Loch Loon increased as he got older and his son came into the business.

Fourth of July at the lodge was a special Scottish American blend of bagpipes and fireworks. In addition to the usual gathering of family for holiday fun and food, the men would gather for late-night card games and plenty of Angus's personal favorite, Glenturret single-malt Scotch whiskey. The card games included two Scottish favorites, Clobyosh (or Clob) and Bela, as well as five-card stud poker. Regardless of the game, the winner was usually the same. His neighbors used to joke that losing money on the card table to Angus was part of their tuition to this homey mountain refuge that he had created for them and their families. After winning their money on the card table, Angus invariably invoked an old Gaelic expression, "Mony a mickle makes a muckle"—pennies add up to dollars. It always got a laugh from the losers.

William had never known his grandmother. In fact, he never even saw a photograph of her. She apparently had tired of the long lonely hours at home with her only child waiting for her husband to leave the office. Once her son had grown up and left for college, she left, too. If anyone knew where she went, they never said. Angus removed every picture of her from their New York apartment and the vacation house on the lake. He refused to talk about her or to let anyone else mention her in his hearing. Even William's father was not allowed to talk about his mother.

Some of William's fondest memories were of summers spent as a child in the home on the lake that his grandfather had built for William's father. While Leod had followed his father into the company, one of the first things the younger man did was to legally change his name from Leod to Leo. Whether he did it to denounce his Scottish roots or merely adopt the name most people called him anyway, this action hurt his father's feelings.

Like his father, Leo was now spending more time in Manhattan while Angus was winding down and spending more and more time at the lake with his grandson.

William worshipped his grandfather, who always called the boy by a Scottish nickname, Willum. While he'd heard some stories of Angus's tenacity and absenteeism, it was not the man he saw. William knew his grandfather as the man who first took him fishing, taught him how to swim, row a boat, play tennis, hit a golf ball, think, and express himself. His grandfather always made time for him and was there to teach him about life. His grandfather was more than patient with him and won the boy's confidence and respect as well. Angus never talked down to his grandson and always treated him like a young man. William thought of his grandfather as God-like and wondered if there was anything the man didn't know or couldn't do.

To young William, Angus seemed to be one with the lake itself, as if he drew inner strength from its deep waters and moved in harmony with its seasons. Angus seemed to know all of the lake's secrets, which he revealed to the boy one at a time. He knew where the fish lived and how to catch them. He knew what creatures made their homes on the lake and how to protect them.

Angus taught William that the lake had loud times, when the winds would stir up its surface, and quiet times, when, if you listened carefully, "you could hear your soul."

In the morning, grandfather and grandson would often row to the deepest part of the lake, lift oars, and drift in silence, letting their thoughts go where they would. Angus taught him what the old man called Scottish meditation.

"Any thoughts are fair, Willum," he said. "Memories of the past or dreams of the future. By becoming one with nature, you can find inner peace while turning problems into opportunities."

In William's fourteenth summer, his relationship with his grandfather reached a new level. Many of Angus's close friends were gone, and the old man spent more and more time on the lake with the boy. He also began talking Gaelic to his grandson, just as he had done with his friends from the old country, trying to pass the ancient language along to his only grandchild.

That summer the old man, for the first time, turned rowing over to his grandson. He loved to sit in the stern of the little rowboat as the sun was setting. He told William that this was called the gloaming, "the tid o day when it is nae fell daurk thareout, but the sun is nae up." Sometimes as William rowed, his grandfather would hum or sing some of the old Scottish songs, like "The Shores of Loch Lomond" or the old man's favorite, "Roamin' in the Gloamin'."

It was as if the old man felt an urgency to download things to his grandson that he felt the boy should know. He gave William endless advice on life and competition:

"Failing means yer playin'" and "Gie it laldy," which meant, do it with gusto.

One night late in the summer, Angus broke the silence about his long-lost wife. "She was a bonnie lass, my Katie McBride. I loved her very much but took her for granted. She went away with a doctor friend of one of our neighbors. They moved to a town near Chicago. She left our forest lake for a new life in Lake Forest—can you believe it?" the old man said with a hint of both laughter and sadness in his eyes.

"I couldn't come to grips with my own role in her departure, so I just tore up her pictures and pretended she'd died."

"Do you still love her, Grandpa?"

"Pride can be a bad thing, Willum, especially when it costs you something very dear to you. A wise man learns to keep his priorities in order." The old man sighed. "I got a note from a friend telling me she died last winter."

"Have you told my father about Grandma McKay?" William asked.

"Naw, laddie, jest ye," Angus said. He gave the boy a stern look. "Remember, what's said on the boat, stays on the boat."

"Yes, Grandfather."

The old man's face softened again. "It's gotten black as the Earl of Hell's waistcoat and I'm pure done in now. Let's go back to the dock."

Months later, on a late-winter day not long before he turned fifteen years old, William got a call at boarding school from his father. Angus had passed away.

The boy's first reaction to the shock and pain of hearing of his grandfather's death was anger . . . anger at his father for being the bearer of this bad news. Then he went to bed that night praying to God that he would wake up in the morning and find out that it was all a bad dream. He cried himself to sleep.

He awoke to find that it hadn't been a bad dream. His grandpa was dead. He vowed then never to talk to God again.

There was a stately service at Fifth Avenue Presbyterian Church in Manhattan. As light snow fell gently outside, a large choir filled the magnificent sanctuary with Angus's favorite Scottish hymns: "A Mighty Fortress Is Our God" and "Glorious Things of Thee Are Spoken."

There was a small reception at the Anglers Club on Broad Street, where the boy sat feeling lost and alone. He felt like crying, but his father had taught him long ago that crying was for babies and sissies, so he didn't.

That summer, William's father moved the family into Angus's house on the lake. On the Friday of Independence Day weekend, his father invited the boy to row out into the middle of the lake where, with the small boat shrouded in silence, Leo took out a small urn from a canvas boat bag and scattered Angus's ashes on the still waters of Loch Loon. There were no prayers and no conversation, no words at all. William noted that his father didn't seem to be spreading Angus's ashes, but rather dumping them as if to get rid of him. Rowing back to shore, the boy turned his head so that his father wouldn't see the tears running down his cheeks.

The holiday weekend went on as if nothing had happened. No one said anything about Angus, so William didn't, either. Unknowingly, the boy was learning the stoic and repressed self-discipline of his Scottish Presbyterian forbears. William didn't pick up a fishing rod that summer or for many summers thereafter.

Soon after Angus's death, the club on Loch Loon was disbanded and the resplendent lodge sat vacant for many years until William, as a grown-up, had it remodeled and turned it into a comfortable restaurant that was now known as the Turtle, a favorite of the locals.

William went on to college, then to the war in Vietnam, before finally joining the family business. A year later, his mother was dying and his father, taking after Grandma McKay, disappeared.

Now, as William reached the middle of the lake, he thought how quickly time goes by. He was the "old man of Loch Loon." He lifted his oars and listened to the lake as his grandfather had taught him to do. A parade of memories coursed through his mind before he settled on one: a day thirty-seven years ago, after William had taken over leadership of his family's investment company, the first day of a week that had forever changed his life.

CHAPTER 2

NEW YORK CITY—1976

William had always felt lonely. An only child packed off to boarding school when he was eight, losing his beloved grandfather as a teenager, followed by his father's abandonment, his mother's death, and a failed marriage: the old feelings returned to the grown man sitting behind his big mahogany desk in his eighteenth-floor corner office looking down on the busy downtown streets of New York City's financial district. A glass of Glenturret single-malt Scotch, his grandfather's favorite drink, in his hand, William gazed at the commuters scurrying to get home and the early diners and theatergoers trying to wave down one of the fleet of yellow cabs driven by a small army of swarthy men from other countries, most of whom could barely speak English and couldn't have cared less.

His dark-wood-paneled office spoke volumes about his success and prominence as interpreted by the tall, curvaceous, middle-aged interior designer whom he had retained and also slept with about five years before. Floor-to-ceiling windows created two walls that gave him breathtaking views of the city. The third wall was covered by bookshelves displaying his military medals, sports trophies, and assorted favorite books. The office was large but not cavernous and tastefully appointed with handsome antique furniture—old but sturdy. His visitors sat on brown leather armchairs, a large comfy couch, or one of six wooden armchairs arrayed around his small round conference table. A beautiful Persian rug appeared to have been made for its space. The focal point of his lair covered the fourth wall, a giant built-in saltwater aquarium. Inside the tank swam four sleek blacktip sharks, the largest of which was almost four feet long. The low backlighting of the aquarium and the slow rhythm of the circling sharks created an intimidating eeriness, heightened by the black eyes of the captive creatures keeping watch over the office and its occupant.

To the world, William McKay seemed to be cool and calmly in charge, the master of his domain. A handsome six foot two with sandy-blond hair just beginning to gray at the temples and steely blue eyes, William worked out hard every day in his private gym or on the squash courts of the uptown New York Racquet and Tennis Club. If he was at all concerned about his thirty-sixth birthday coming up in two months, he never showed it.

Success had come easy to William, first on the playing fields at Phillips Academy Andover, later at the Military Academy at West Point, then as the army's youngest Special Forces battalion commander in Vietnam, and now as one of the foremost stock traders on Wall Street taking full advantage of his seat on the New York Stock Exchange. The elite brokerage firm founded by his grandfather had grown to more than 120 professionals.

William had tried his hand at marriage, after he returned home from 'Nam, to a girl named June whom he'd met at a mixer in high school. The ceremony was beautiful. He wore his army dress blues. They honeymooned in Jamaica, and he set his bride up in a starter house in Stamford, Connecticut. He thought this marriage would be the end to his loneliness.

It wasn't long before William found that he had fallen in love with his new profession and out of love with his bride, if they'd ever been in love at all. He worked later and later hours in Manhattan. As for June, she realized that she was more in love with the idea of being married than being with William.

The marriage lasted less than a year. William suggested that they return the wedding gifts. She told him "over my dead body." Her father, a prominent attorney in Darien, helped get the marriage annulled. William gave her the house and the wedding gifts, many of which were still unopened.

A decade later, William was to be honored as New York City's youngest ever Under Forty Executive of the Year by the chamber of commerce at a black-tie dinner at the Waldorf Astoria, a reward for his work as an adviser to a bunch of rich fat cats, helping them become even richer. *How strange life is*, William thought. Twelve years before, the army had called him an adviser as well, while leading his men through jungles in Vietnam, trying to kill the Cong before they killed him or his men. He had "advised" these young men on how to stay alive. If they failed to heed his advice, he'd sit in his quarters with pen and paper "advising" their parents of their sons' deaths. It was the loneliest he'd felt in his lonely life. When he returned home in uniform from the unpopular war, he'd been spit upon by angry war protestors at JFK airport. Tonight he was being honored by New York's aristocracy.

This evening he would not be alone. He would be accompanied by his young fiancée, Stacy Bryant. He knew that she would be beautifully turned out after spending the afternoon at Vidal Sassoon having her long blond hair trimmed and a mani/pedi after a morning of fittings of the new navy-blue, sequined frock from Bergdorf Goodman that she had chosen for the event. She would turn heads. She always did—drawing looks of lust from the men and envy from the women, many of whom had spent their days carpooling in Connecticut.

He thought about her as he walked to the bar in his credenza, put some fresh ice cubes in his glass, and poured himself another Glenturret. Twenty-nine years old, the girl had a fine pedigree to go along with her willowy good looks. Educated first at Rye Country Day School, she had captained the girl's lacrosse team and starred in many of the school's theatricals. Her mediocre grades, bolstered by her doting daddy's money, were more than enough to gain her admission to Smith College, where she majored in art history. After graduation she'd worked at Sotheby's, advancing her knowledge in American art before moving to a small boutique gallery store on Seventy-Ninth Street.

It was there that they'd met on a warm fall Saturday morning a year and a half ago, while William was browsing in search of a small antique polo bronze for his new apartment on Eighty-First.

The attraction was mutual, strong, and immediate. They met for dinner that night at one of William's favorite restaurants, Giovanni's on the Upper East Side, for Italian food and shared a bottle of delicious Chianti.

It would have seemed unnatural if they hadn't ended up back in William's apartment, tossing their clothes around his bedroom and making passionate love on his queen-sized bed without bothering to throw back his silver fox bedspread. She ravished him. Never before had William experienced anything like her hunger and inventiveness. Thinking of it now, he smiled despite himself. It was a sad smile.

He was snapped out of his reverie by the voice of his longtime assistant, Arnelle Whitten, on his intercom. "Mr. Prescott to see you, sir," she said in her gentle island accent.

Arnelle, a beautiful and cheerful Bajan woman, had been with him since he'd started at the firm more than eleven years ago, with the exception of eight months when she had moved back to her native Barbados to play house with her island lover, James somebody. Apparently the experience hadn't gone well. She'd cried when she came to beg for her job back. William had tried to appear sympathetic but was inwardly delighted that she was coming back to him. In the time she'd been gone, her replacement, an airhead named Doreen, had all but undone Arnelle's excellent filing system while decimating the office's efficiency and raising her boss's stress level to the highest level, what the military called DEFCON 1. Now Arnelle was back with a healthy hatred for all men except William.

Taking a thick eight-by-ten-inch mailing envelope marked CONFIDENTIAL from atop his desk and sliding it into a drawer, William said, "Thank you, Arnelle, please send him in."

Randall Prescott, his brilliant young protégé, walked into his office carrying a blue folder under his arm. A thin, good-looking young man in his early thirties with dark hair and brown eyes, he always looked like he was stepping out of a Hugo Boss ad in *GQ* magazine, which William was sure he read religiously. On his job application, Randall had claimed to have been on the undergraduate fencing team at Yale before moving on to Harvard Law School, where he graduated in the top of his class.

"Good evening, Mr. McKay. I've got some papers for you to sign."

"Thank you, Randy," William replied. "Just leave them on my desk, if you don't mind. I'll sign them tomorrow."

"As you wish, sir," he said, putting the folder down. "And by the way, congratulations again on the wonderful award you will be receiving this evening. I'm really excited to be introducing you at the dinner."

"Not too long I hope, Randy." William smiled.

"No, sir," Randall said. "I know your preference for brevity and have tried to keep it short, but it wasn't easy given all you've accomplished."

"My career's not over yet, Randy," William said.

"I know, sir. You're still a young man."

William wondered if the term *brownnoser* was still in vogue.

"The committee asked me to pick out a commemorative gift for you. I hope you'll like it. Miss Bryant helped me choose it. She has wonderful taste."

"Thank you, Randy," William said as his young associate started toward the door. "By the way, Randy, as my attorney, do you think you should draft a prenuptial agreement for me and Stacy to sign?"

"It's always a good idea for anyone getting married. And, sir, if I may speak plainly, you are a very wealthy man. But it's also true that your fiancée seems to be a wonderful woman, who I understand comes from a family of wealth and privilege, which she is in line to inherit, so perhaps a document is unnecessary in this instance."

"Randy, do I strike you as a happy person?"

Randall was visibly taken aback. "I'm not sure what you mean, sir."

"Happiness, Randy. I'm sure you've read about it somewhere."

Randall barked a nervous laugh. "You seem to be happy when Stacy is around."

William nodded. "Stacy wishes I was happier. She thinks I should smile more . . . thinks I should open my heart and be more trusting of people."

"Sir?"

"I've been married before. I have no children, at least not yet. My mother died when I was quite a bit younger than you, and I haven't spoken to my father in over ten years. I have no heir and no logical successor. So what would you do if you were in my shoes?"

Randall thought for a minute, then said, "Again speaking candidly, sir, I believe that lesser men would need a prenuptial."

"Lesser men?" William asked.

"When I think of all you've achieved and all I've learned from you, I just don't see you that way."

"What way is that, Randy?"

"You're deliberate and decisive. You determine what you want and you commit to doing whatever it takes to get it. I've learned that from you. You've never been one to hedge your bets."

"Interesting," William said. "That gives me something to think about."

"I only want to help, sir," Randall said, "and if you want me to draft a prenup for you, I'll do it. You know I'm always looking after your best interests as if they were my own."

"I know, Randy, and it really helps me sleep nights," William said with a smirk Prescott didn't seem to notice.

"Will there be anything else, sir?"

"No, thanks, Randy," William said, turning back to his desk. "I'll see you tonight."

"Yes, sir," Randall said, turning to leave.

For eight years, Randall Prescott had served William well. Demonstrating an outstanding blend of legal acumen and high energy, he had assumed more and more corporate responsibility, eventually taking over many of his boss's personal affairs. But lately, William had begun to find Prescott an irritant. It wasn't his unctuous pandering or his transparent patronizing that was causing William's growing mistrust. Tonight, William had finally figured out what it was.

Feeling a growing sense of anger along with the warm glow of the whiskey, William poured himself another drink and stepped into his personal bathroom to change for dinner.

Closing the door behind him, he stripped off his clothes, turned on the hot water in the basin, and shaved. When he finished, he splashed cold water on his face and took a close look at himself in the mirror. He knew the circles under his eyes were from not sleeping very well lately. He also noticed how his summer tan was all but gone, leaving him looking rather pale and gaunt. *Maybe it's time to head south for some sun*, he thought as he stepped over to the shower and turned on the water.

He picked up his half-full glass from the counter and carried it into the tiled shower. Holding his drink in one hand, he turned up the volume of hot water as high as he could stand it. As the shower door steamed over, he stood for a long, long time with water cascading down his neck and shoulders.

Closing his eyes, he took a deep drink hoping that the whiskey would chase away the sense of loneliness that was welling up again in his heart. Now with the glass almost drained, he turned the temperature as low as he could stand it and felt reinvigorated.

After a few minutes, William turned off the water, stepped out of the shower, and toweled off.

He began dressing in the clothes that Arnelle had laid out for him. He liked the feel of the lightly starched, white, pleated formal shirt as he pulled it over his shoulders. His acuity a bit dulled by the whiskey, William fumbled a bit with his shirt's studs and cuff links but made fast work of tying the dreaded bow tie that befuddled so many of his male friends. Black tuxedo pants, suspenders, socks, and formal black wing tips and he felt almost ready to face the world.

As he walked out into his office, tuxedo jacket over his arm, his intercom buzzed again. "It's eight o'clock, Mr. MacKay. Bernard is here," Arnelle's voice said, announcing William's tailor.

"Thanks, Arnelle."

"If you don't mind, I'm going to head over to the Waldorf now for the banquet. I don't want to be late. I don't want you to be late, either."

"You get going. And don't worry, I'll be there. Please send Bernard in."

"Don't keep Bernard too long, either. He's my date for tonight."

William filled his glass again as Bernard entered the room.

"Good evening, sir," he said in his distinctive Scottish brogue.

"How are you, Bernard? Long time no see."

"It has been a long time, sir. I know how hard you've been working."

"And tonight they give me my prize," William said as he stepped onto the small wooden stool that Bernard had brought with him, swaying just a bit.

A slight man, Bernard Stewart, a widower with two grown-up sons, was probably in his eighties. He was bald but for a rim of white hair, and his shoulders always seemed to be stooped over, no doubt an occupational hazard for tailors. Bernard deftly threaded a needle and started stitching the hemline of William's pants.

William focused on the circling sharks.

"I remember when your father won this award thirty-six years ago. I trimmed his suit as he stood on this very stool."

"Was he happy?"

"If my memory serves me, sir, he behaved very much like you are behaving tonight."

"Like father, like son, eh, Bernard? When I took over this company, I had to make some big decisions. We had to embrace technology. People who'd been here for years couldn't change. They had to be let go. We needed to innovate to be competitive."

"These are things I know little of," said the old tailor.

After a short silence, William asked, "Bernard, what would you do differently, if you could do it all over again?"

Bernard thought for a moment. "My boys—I wish that I'd spent more time with them. That's time that you can never get back."

William said nothing.

"What about you, sir?" Bernard asked.

William just shook his head.

CHAPTER 3

LOCH LOON—2012

As William reached the middle of the lake, he reminded himself that today he was on a special mission. For the next two weeks his daughter, Sarah, his only child, and her twelve-year-old son, Kyle, would be staying at the cottage across the lake.

Sarah had been a joy growing up, a little blond-haired, blue-eyed bundle of energy and curiosity. She seemed born to the natural world. She couldn't learn enough about the outdoors and its creatures, many of whom she befriended or adopted. From a very early age, all things in her world—trees, flowers, plants, and animals—had to have names. It sent her mom and dad scurrying to Barnes and Noble to buy reference books so that they could answer her questions.

William would never forget the look on her face the first time he took her fishing at the lake and she caught a tiny little multicolored sunfish. She cried tears of joy when she released it so that she could see it again another day.

William knew that he had a fishing buddy for life.

Sarah's curiosity served her well in the classroom, where she was an honors student throughout grade school and high school. William harbored some hopes early on that this bright young girl might choose a financial career and join him in the firm. He'd even thought about changing the company's name to McKay and Daughter. While it was a nice pipe dream, William knew it wouldn't happen. When he mentioned finance to his daughter, her eyes glazed over. Science and English literature were her passions. Her extracurricular activities did not include sports, but rather journalism and theater. Her senior year, she was editor of the school newspaper and produced a one-act musical for the drama club titled *The McKays of Loch Loon*. William remembered watching his daughter's musical with pride not only in her accomplishment, but also in her appreciation of their beautiful family retreat. He laughed along with the audience when some of the young actors came on stage for the finale wearing kilts.

William was not surprised that his daughter chose to pursue a career in journalism at Syracuse University and wondered if its proximity to Loch Loon had influenced her. While at Syracuse as a freshman, she met and fell in love with a senior named Peter Daniels. William found the boy difficult to talk to from the first time they met. It seemed his only interest was movies, old and new, and he seemed to spend most of his time lying around watching them on television.

After Peter graduated, the two eloped to Los Angeles. Sarah was only eighteen. William was concurrently shocked and infuriated. Selfishly, he feared losing the precious time he spent with Sarah at Loch Loon, although she vowed that, no matter how far away she was living, she would always return to the Adirondacks for at least two weeks every summer.

It wasn't until three months later that William learned that there had been extenuating circumstances. When the couple had taken off for the West Coast, his daughter was four months pregnant . . . pregnant with a child conceived on a recreational midwinter liaison at the family homestead at Loch Loon.

To give Peter credit, he did seem to take good care of Sarah, and after a few years of financial struggles, he provided her and their son, Kyle, with a comfortable lifestyle by writing television scripts—all bad television scripts in William's mind.

Sarah had kept her promise to visit Loch Loon every summer, always with Kyle and sometimes with Peter. William would also take his daughter to dinner when he was on the Left Coast, but he missed having her close by and having the chance to watch his grandson grow up. Kyle loved his fishing trips on the lake with his grandpa as much as his grandpa did. William saw in the boy's eyes the same look of wonderment that he'd seen in Sarah's eyes. He knew that it was the same feeling he'd had when he was Kyle's age fishing with his own grandfather.

A month ago, Peter had announced that he no longer wanted to be married. Reluctantly, Sarah had agreed to a trial separation. She arrived at Loch Loon the previous day with Kyle.

Sarah confided in her dad that the news had been tough on her teenage son, who had withdrawn into a shell, refusing to talk to anyone. She asked her father if he'd take the boy fishing to see if Kyle might open up to him. Today William was to add fishing guide/psychologist to his role of grandpa. He knew it would be challenging. He thought to himself that he knew a lot more about fish than kids, but he was willing to give it a try.

Parenting was a learned skill that you perfected through trial and error, William thought. Just when you thought you might be getting it right, the children were grown up and gone. Then you stored the skills away, only to bring them out, dust them off, and try them again on grandchildren.

William loved his grandson and had wonderful memories of their summers fishing together on Loch Loon.

He tried to remember how his grandfather had treated him. If he could draw on those lessons, he might be able to help his own grandson.

About a hundred feet from the shoreline, he looked over his shoulder and saw his pretty daughter standing on a small dock in her bathrobe. Next to her, Kyle slouched in baggy hip-hop jeans, a hooded sweatshirt, and frosted hair, engrossed in some handheld device. This was not the happy, cheerful young boy that William knew.

"Hi, Dad," Sarah called out.

"Hey, Minnow," William said, using the nickname he had coined for her years ago.

"Say hello to your grandpa, Kyle," Sarah said. The boy was oblivious, lost in his video game. She gave him a poke in the ribs.

"What?" the boy said, annoyed.

"Your grandfather's here," she said, louder. Kyle glanced up before returning to his game. William smiled for his daughter's sake. "How 'bout grabbing the bowline, Kyle?"

"The what?" Kyle scowled, not budging an inch.

Sarah brushed by her son, grabbed the bowline, pulled the little dinghy snug to the dock, and deftly secured the line to a cleat. Stepping back, she picked up a small cooler that she handed to her father.

"Sandwiches and my homemade potato salad. Beer for you, soda for him."

Great, William thought, *it may be quiet out there today, but at least I won't starve to death.*

"Thanks, honey," he said, stowing the cooler. "How about Kyle and I meet you and your mom at the Turtle at six?"

Sarah nodded.

"Ready to do some fishing, my boy?" William asked Kyle.

"Nah."

Sarah elbowed Kyle in the ribs. "Whatever," he said, stepping into the boat.

"What's that contraption in your hand?" William asked.

"It's a Nintendo DS," the boy said. "People in the twenty-first century play games on them."

"May I see it please?"

Kyle handed the video game to his grandfather, who examined the small device in his strong, suntanned old hands.

"Fascinating," he said, "but why are you attempting to bring it on my boat?"

"It will keep me from dying of boredom," Kyle shot back.

William paused, looked at the device again, and a faint smile came to his face.

"Contraband, my boy," he said, handing the video game to Sarah. He looked his grandson in the eye. "You can do one or the other, but you can't do both. Not on my boat."

The boy scowled.

"Now get your butt on board," William said. "We are about to embark on a great adventure." Hearing his own words, William knew he sounded like an old fossil, or worse.

Kyle rolled his eyes as he sat down on the small bench seat in the stern of the boat. Sarah undid the line and tossed it to her dad, who gave her a wink. He pushed off, rowing the boat into the lifting fog as Kyle slouched in the backseat.

William rowed in silence. After fifteen minutes, the boy glanced at his grandfather, exhaled deeply, and continued brooding.

Ten minutes later, William broke the silence. "I've known quite a few brooders over the years, and I can tell you with some certainty that you are a talent."

"I'm not brooding," Kyle said.

"Oh really?" the old man asked. "Then what are you doing, pouting? The Lord hates a pouter."

"I'm thinking."

"Of course you are, my boy."

"I'm not a boy," Kyle said.

"I can see that," William said. "Looks like you're almost ready to start shaving."

"I'm not a kid anymore."

"What's on your mind, son?"

"Why should I tell you anything?" he said. "Adults don't understand."

"Understand what?"

"You say you want us to grow up to be good adults, then you lie to us every chance you get."

"That's a pretty wide-ranging indictment."

"So you never lie?"

"No," William said. "I try not to; though I think we grown-ups do shade the truth sometimes."

"Why?"

"I think it's because we don't want our children to be hurt and also because we know we're not perfect and don't want our children to see or know that."

"So lying's okay then?" Kyle asked.

"I didn't say that," William answered.

The boat floated on. Grandson and grandfather stared off in different directions. Finally, William said, "Would you like to hear a story?"

"Not really," Kyle answered.

"But you used to like my stories."

"I told you, I'm not a kid anymore," the boy said.

"Clearly."

"You're patronizing me."

Impressed by his grandson's command of the language and the fact that he seemed to be on the verge of opening up a little, William stopped rowing, letting the little boat drift silently over the calm surface of the lake. "Big word for a twelve-year-old, Kyle," he said.

"See, you did it again. I don't need to hear some old fairy tale." The boy stared down at his feet then looked his grandfather in the eye. "I'm not interested in your *On Golden Pond* bonding crap."

"Interesting movie. Did you see it?"

"My dad did. It's what he calls this place." Kyle stared off into the distance. "What's the difference? He's just another adult who lies to kids. He didn't even have the courage to tell me he was leaving. Left me a note and took off."

The boy's sadness and anger gripped William's heart. The boat drifted on in silence.

"Since you've made it clear that you don't want to hear a fairy tale, I think maybe a true story might be in order. I won't tell you any lies, okay?"

Kyle looked into his grandfather's eyes. With a small smirk, he said, "How 'bout telling me a man's story? What about that scar on your forehead? Why don't you tell me how you got it?"

William touched the old scar. "That's a long and probably inappropriate story."

"We've got all day," Kyle said, "and I told you I'm not a kid anymore. I can handle it."

"You really want to hear about it?"

"I do."

"All right," William said. "You told me the truth about how you felt about your dad's leaving. But first you need to make your old granddad a promise. What's said on the boat, stays on the boat. That's the fishermen's code."

THE
GLENTURRE

CHAPTER 4

NEW YORK CITY—1976

By the time William had his tuxedo on, he had a little buzz on—or, as his Scottish ancestors would have said, "he was pissed."

He went down the elevator into the cold night air, forgetting to put on his overcoat. His chauffeur, Shay, pulled up in his limousine, and his doorman, Fritz, opened the rear passenger-side door for him.

As the limo pulled away from the curb, Shay looked at him in the rearview mirror. "Are you okay, sir?"

"Top of the world," William said, trying mightily not to slur his words. "If I were any better, I'd cancel my life insurance!"

Traffic was horrible, but William didn't care. He had a fully stocked bar in the limo. He was late and had missed the cocktail hour, but it didn't matter. When he arrived at the Waldorf, William was greeted by an old guy named Devon Mills, a guy who seemed to serve in perpetuity as the chairman of the chamber of commerce.

Obviously relieved by his arrival, Devon shook his hand and said, "Good evening, William. You're a little bit late so I'll escort you to the ballroom myself. Our guests are beginning to be seated, and you will be next to me on the dais. Your fiancée, Miss Bryant, is already here."

They walked down the hall and through the doors of one of the most beautiful ballrooms in New York. While he'd been here many times, he'd never seen it so filled with people—men in their tuxedos, women in their gowns. It didn't matter. He knew that they weren't here for him, but rather to hobnob—to see and be seen and maybe get their pictures in the *New York Times*.

And anyway, William had a buzz on.

He got to his seat and Stacy, looking beautiful as always, stood up and gave him an air-kiss on each cheek, being careful that their faces never touched for fear of smudging her makeup. Seated next to her, on the other side, was William's young legal protégé, Randall Bowen Prescott. He liked everyone to call him Randall, so William, naturally, called him Randy. Randy jumped to his feet and started shaking William's hand as if his arm were a pump handle. *What a dork,* William thought. Next to him was some kind of priest or bishop or rabbi or something, here to bore everyone with the mandatory pre-meal grace. Feeling rather out of focus and still disenfranchised by religion for letting his grandfather and mother die, not to mention so many of his men in

Vietnam, William ignored the clergyman and what he had to say.

The minute they were seated, Devon Mills stepped to the microphone, welcomed the crowd, and noted how happy the chamber was to honor the first son of a prior awardee. The guy with the white collar said grace. When he'd finished, Mills got up again, promised to return to the mike soon, and wished everyone bon appétit.

The meal held little interest for William so he ordered another single-malt whiskey on ice, and then a double. He caught a look of disdain from his fiancée but could not have cared less. As people chatted on mindlessly all around him, he remembered ignoring them and scanning the Grand Ballroom itself. He'd forgotten, or perhaps never noticed, how beautiful it was, the only two-tiered ballroom in New York City, with a ceiling that must have been more than forty feet high. The beautifully decorated elegance of this iconic venue was illuminated by a huge custom-made chandelier.

Just then, old Devon bounced to the microphone again and introduced Randall, who got up, took some notes out of his vest pocket, cleared his throat, and started to ramble. William wasn't sure what all he said, or maybe anything he didn't say, but he did remember Randall throwing around a bunch of big words. Perhaps his speech was designed to win him future consideration for this award—or more aptly Devon Mills's job after the old geezer croaked.

Smiling to himself, William tried to focus on Randall's speech.

". . . businessman, mentor, leader, uncompromising vision"—blah, blah, blah—"philanthropist, patron of the arts, collector of antiquities"—blah, blah, blah—"embodies the idea of honor, teaches every day that life without honor would be useless."

Then finally, "And so as a symbol of that honor, I'd like to present him with this gift—which, by the way, ladies and gentlemen, I picked out for him with a little help from his lovely fiancée, Stacy Bryant. So without further ado, it is my pleasure to introduce the Under Forty Executive of the Year, Mr. William McKay."

William was vaguely aware of the huge well-heeled crowd exploding to their feet in a standing ovation as he himself struggled to stand up. Randall gave him a rosewood box and looked at him quizzically.

William tried to focus as the smiling crowd settled in. First thing he did was tap three times on the microphone, just to make sure it was working. What a noise! Sounded like three gunshots echoing through the crowded hall. *That'll get their attention*, William thought.

"Well, well, well, let's see what Randy got me," he started out.

He ran his hand across the smooth rosewood box, opened the lid to find two beautiful, perfectly preserved, gold inlaid French dueling pistols complete with a silver powder flask, a velvet pouch full of lead ball ammunition, cloth wadding, and a filigree tin of percussion caps. He'd seen pistols like these at West Point and even had a chance to load and fire one on the practice range.

And at that moment, he knew where his speech was going.

Looking out at the crowd he said, "Dueling pistols, French, eighteenth century, Normandy region I believe."

The urbane crowd murmured approvingly.

"Thank you, Randy," he said. "They are magnificent."

Smiling widely, Randall answered, "All original, perfectly preserved and maintained."

"And functional?" William asked.

"I believe so."

"Fantastic," William responded, bringing the pistols to half cock as he began his acceptance speech.

"Father whatever your name is, all you politicos out there who got free tickets and distinguished guests who actually paid to be here. Randy spoke of the importance of honor in our lives, and these are truly the weapons of honorable men."

Then right in front of the crowd, still talking, he began loading the pistols, first with gunpowder, then wadding, then lead balls, and finally more wadding. Through his haze, he noticed that the crowd began to murmur more loudly.

He continued, "Because without honor, we lose what is potentially the greatest part of our humanity . . . our ability to trust one another."

He primed each pistol with a percussion cap and continued, "Ladies and gentlemen, this Under Forty Executive of the Year has a problem." He cocked both pistol hammers.

"You see, Randall Bowen Prescott, my honorable and talented young protégé . . . is banging my lovely young bride-to-be, Stacy Bryant. He's probably got his little hand in her panties as we speak."

At this, the murmur turned to a gasp. Randy glanced over to see the clergyman at the head table cross himself.

Must be a Catholic, he thought, . . . *whatever.*

The earlier beautiful Stacy looked mortified and gasped, "William, how could you?"

William smiled at her and said, still over the mike, "I'm not talking to you, Stacy. I'm talking to your sweetie." He thought that this was getting to be fun.

"Now, Randy—I'm sorry, I mean Randall—said in his eloquent introduction something about my teaching by example, so watch closely now; you all may learn something."

The stunned crowd went deadly silent as he walked over and set one of the loaded and cocked dueling pistols on the tabletop right in front of Randy and next to his half-drunk glass of red wine.

"Randy," he went on, "you have disgraced both my honor and your own. Now in front of your peers, I am challenging you to a duel to the death."

The once arrogant and cocky Randall turned as white as his tuxedo shirt. "I, I, um . . . You can't be serious."

"Oh, but I am, Randall. As serious as death, and you've given me the wrong answer. Show these people how honorable you are. Pick up that gun and show 'em what you're made of. Or are you some kind of . . . lesser man?"

"I, I, I don't know what to say," Randall whispered.

Feeling his anger boil again, William said, almost shouting, his face now but inches from Randall's ear as he stared straight ahead into the crowd, "Where is your honor now, pal? Did you think it was just a word? Pick up the fuckin' gun. Now!"

William's drunkenness disappeared in an instant—he felt the way he had in the army before combat. He watched as sweat beaded up on Randall's forehead and his lower lip began to tremble.

At the other end of the head table, Devon Mills jumped to his feet and up to the microphone.

"Mr. McKay, as chairman of the chamber of commerce, I must demand that you stop this outburst!"

"What'd you say to me?" William asked, still in a cool rage.

Dropping his voice, Devon said, "I understand that you believe there may have been some type of indiscretion, but this behavior is inappropriate."

"Some type of indiscretion?"

"Please, William," Devon said in a loud whisper, "you're making a terrible spectacle of yourself."

"Fine, Devon," William said, tucking the rosewood box under his arm and walking off the stage with a cocked dueling pistol in each hand. "Give your award to someone else . . . I'll keep the guns." And with that, he headed down the center aisle for the exit. When he reached the big double doors, he turned around and shouted, "Oh, by the way. Randall, you're fired, and Stacy, the wedding's off, but I'll send you a copy of the detective's report. I'm sure you'll love the pictures."

And with that, he turned away from the beautiful women and handsome men, and walked out the door.

Shay was waiting for him in the car. Oblivious, Shay said, "Did you have a pleasant evening, sir?"

William chuckled despite himself.

"Yes, thank you, Shay, it was satisfying."

"Home then, sir?" Shay said.

"No, Shay, I'd like you to drop me off at my office."

Arriving at the building, William carried the dueling pistols, now back in the rosewood box, through the lobby, waving to Luis, the nighttime security man, as he walked by his counter behind which on the wall were the burnished bronze letters MCKAY AND SON. At the eighteenth floor he was greeted by the hum of a floor buffer as the cleaning crew went about their nightly routine.

As he reached the double doors to his office suite, he fumbled a bit with his keys, then walked through the darkened reception area, past Arnelle's desk, and into his office, never bothering to turn on the incandescent lights. The phone on his desk was ringing. He put the rosewood box on his desk and turned on the soft background lights of the aquarium and the light in his bar. That was all he'd need.

He thought about ignoring the ring, but realized that he'd ignored too many things in his life. He picked it up and growled into the receiver, "What?"

The sweet Bajan-flavored voice of Arnelle said, "Are you all right, sir?"

"Yeah, Arnelle, I'm fine," he said, "just had to get a few things off my chest."

"Do you want me to come over?" she asked. "Is there anything I can do for you?"

"No, Arnelle, thanks. I'm fine. Don't worry about me." Then he said, "I made a real ass of myself, didn't I?"

There was a pause on the phone before Arnelle replied. "Well, you livened up a rather boring event, but as we say at home, 'you gave de devil his due.' You should have seen Randall and Stacy trying to slink out of the room! I said good-bye to them and they ignored me. What a pair. I never liked either of them. They deserve each other."

"Maybe so," William said, "but I feel like going into hiding."

"You hold your head high. You're a good man, William," Arnelle said, calling him by his first name for the first time. "Are you sure you don't want me to come over there?"

"No, but thanks, Arnelle," he said. "You just go home now. I'll be fine."

The phone call ended. William poured himself a stiff drink of whiskey, took off his coat and shoes, and loosened his tie. Then he put Nat King Cole on his turntable: "Unforgettable." As the music played, William sat down at his desk and mused on the events of the night. *Unforgettable*, he thought, *yeah, that's what I was tonight.*

Then things got kind of weird.

William climbed up on his desk with the two fully cocked dueling pistols, one in each hand. He looked over at the largest shark in the aquarium, and the creature seemed to look back at him. He pointed one of the loaded pistols at the shark and as it circled, so did William, turning and turning, trying to end up with the pistol pointing at the shark as it passed closest to the glass.

Suddenly, the record skipped. This distracted him. He felt dizzy, lost his balance, and fell off his desk, hitting the floor hard on his shoulder, causing one of the guns to go off. The lead ball grazed his forehead and lodged itself in the office ceiling.

When he came to, ten minutes later, he could smell the gunpowder hanging in the air. He sat up on the office floor and looked around; the record was still skipping and his vision was blurred. Blood ran over his left eye and down his face and onto his shirt. His forehead hurt, and he touched it lightly. A flesh wound, most likely. He looked at his aquarium wall and again watched the sharks swimming in their familiar pattern as if nothing had happened.

• • •

Back on Loch Loon, Grandpa William paused, took two fishing rods from under the gunnel, and started baiting the hooks with worms. Then he looked up and smiled at his now wide-eyed, gaping grandson.

"Holy crap," the boy said. "Are you bullshitting me, Grandpa?"

"Of course not, Kyle."

"Well, what happened then?"

"What do you mean what happened then?" William said. "You asked for a man's story, a story about how I got my scar. That's the story."

"Yeah," the young boy said, "but what happened next? I mean there you are sitting on the floor after just about blowing your own head off!"

"Okay, son, if you need to know, hold on to this rod and I'll tell you," William said, leaning back on his flotation cushion seat.

"So . . . my father called me."

"Wait a minute, Grandpa. My mom told me that you never talked to your father, that he abandoned you and your mother."

"You're right, I didn't. That's the strange part."

CHAPTER 5

THE CALL

The phone on William's desk started ringing. Holding a handkerchief against his forehead so he didn't bleed all over his carpet, he turned off the record, grabbed the half-full bottle of Glenturret, and pressed the speakerphone button.

A gravelly voice on the other end said, "William McKay?"

"Yes," he said. "Is this the police? Is this about what happened earlier?"

The voice said, "No, for Christ's sake. This is not the cops. It's your father."

"My father? You're sure about that?"

"Of course I'm sure. What kind of stupid-ass question is that?"

"Well, I'm sorry," William said. "Should I have been expecting your call? It's been almost eleven years—"

His father's voice cut him off. "Oh, cry me a river, kid. The phone works two ways. I wanted to congratulate you on winning that award."

"Not that it's any of your business, but I refused to accept it."

"What happened, son?" his father said.

"It's a long story and it doesn't concern you," he said, trying to think of the last time his father had called him son.

From the speakerphone Leo McKay's voice said, "Listen, I've got this idea I want to run by you."

"This ought to be good," William said.

"How'd you like to compete in a father-and-son fishing tournament?"

"Against each other?"

"No," he said, "as a team. You and me with my fishing guide against a bunch of other teams."

Through his haze, William couldn't believe his own ears. His father calling after more than a decade of silence asking him to go fishing like nothing at all had happened. Maybe he was dreaming.

"You hear me, kid? You still there?"

"Yeah, I'm still here," William said. *This is too weird*, he thought. Despite his surprise and anger, he was flattered that his father had called him, and despite himself, he felt his competitive McKay juices flowing in the face of a challenge.

"I haven't fished since I was fourteen—"

"Doesn't matter," his father said. "The tournament starts at nine a.m."

"When?" William asked.

"Tomorrow," his father said, repeating, "nine a.m."

"Tomorrow? You must be joking. I just can't . . ."

His father interrupted him again and said, "What do you really have to do? C'mon, kid, you can let the world take a few turns without you. You've got people up there you can trust to do your bidding."

"I'm a little short on trust right now," William said. "And I don't even know where you are."

"I'm at home," his father said.

"Home?" William asked. "I don't know where you live."

"Islamorada," his father said, "down in the Conch Republic."

"The Conch Republic?"

"The Florida Keys . . . Sport-Fishing Capital of the World. You can fly one of your fancy jets into Marathon. Islamorada is only thirty minutes from the airport. Be there at seven fifteen a.m. I'll pick you up. Now, are you in or out?"

William looked around his office at the sharks, the pistols on the floor, the snow falling outside, and heard his own voice saying, "All right, I'm in."

• • •

"But why would you go there, Grandpa?" Kyle interrupted. "The man abandoned you and your mother. Why would you want anything to do with him?"

"Well, Kyle, I thought about that, too, but you know what? He was my father, part of my family. While he hurt me badly, I still wanted to see him again . . . to find out what he was doing and what he was thinking . . . to find out why he left us . . . why he never wrote or called, even after my mother passed away."

"That doesn't make sense, Grandpa," Kyle said.

"I know that, son, but families are families and they don't always make sense. I also knew that the hatred I had inside was tearing me apart. I had to let it go. Perhaps this trip would help me do that. And to tell you the truth, I was embarrassed by what I'd done at the banquet and didn't mind the opportunity to get out of Dodge for a while."

"So what'd you do next?"

"Well, time was wasting. I called my chief pilot and told him to fuel up our jet."

• • •

William didn't even have time to stop at his place for a change of clothes. The only thing he took with him was the rosewood box and pistols. He wasn't sure what he was thinking or if he was even thinking at all. Maybe if his father explained why he'd abandoned his mother and him and apologized, he'd give him the pistols as a house gift, and if he didn't . . . well, maybe he'd challenge him to a duel and shoot him, he thought, as that sad smile came back to his face.

Having released his limo driver for the night, William hailed a cab and clamored into the backseat. The wide-eyed look he got from the young bearded Middle Eastern driver reminded William that he was indeed quite a sight.

The cab sailed over the George Washington Bridge and into New Jersey with no traffic, arriving at Teterboro Airport in no time. He'd given his captain and co-captain only an hour to get ready, and there they were, standing in front of the private aircraft terminal, looking sharp in their winter wear, navy-blue hooded parkas with the company's logo embroidered on the front pocket.

William saw that his cabdriver looked happy for the first time, probably on four counts—to arrive, to get paid, to see him out of his cab, and to get out of there.

Captain Frank Harding said, "Good morning, sir, any luggage?"

"No, Frank," said William, "just me and this wooden box." William knew that his chief pilot was too professional to ask why he was dressed in a bloody tuxedo with no luggage.

"The snow has moved through and we have a beautiful, clear, full-moonlit night for our two-hour-and-forty-five-minute flight to Marathon, Florida, tonight, Mr. McKay," Frank said as they walked to the plane, a twin-engine Gulfstream II corporate jet.

"Thank you, Captain," William said. He knew that Captain Harding wasn't just being polite, but cleverly restating their destination to make sure he hadn't made a mistake or hadn't misheard him over the phone an hour ago.

Before taking off, William asked Captain Harding if he had the experimental mobile phone on board, the one that the head of Motorola had given him to try. The captain said yes and William asked him if he would charge it up en route so he could use it in Florida. "Also," he asked, "when we arrive in Marathon, would you call my office and give Arnelle the phone number so she can reach me if she needs to?"

"Yes, sir," Captain Harding said.

William always loved boarding this plane. The interior had white-and-tan surfaces with comfortable brown leather seats, fold-out polished mahogany tables, and dark faux-mahogany trim. It was laid out with a small forward galley, four seats facing one another, a center dining/meeting table for four, and a three-piece sofa that converted into a bed next to another, somewhat private, removed seat as well as an aft head and rear luggage compartment.

The lavish furnishings actually housed or covered the business equipment that he'd had built into the fuselage. The plane's cabin was equipped with a ticker tape for receiving updated stock quotations, two satellite phones, a fax, and a printer.

Tonight, however, instead of a flying office, it was a crash pad. The last thing William remembered was flopping down into one of the seats, doing up his seat belt, and falling instantly asleep, even before the plane taxied out for takeoff.

CHAPTER 6

THE KEYS

The bright rays of the rising sun hit William square in the eyes, snapping him out of a sound sleep into a massive headache from ear to ear. He touched the wound on his forehead. Two of the gauges on the front bulkhead wall showed that they were flying 380 miles an hour at twelve thousand feet. William squinted to look out the window. Below he saw a desolate expanse of shallow water of intermittent shades of blue, green, and brown. It reminded him of an old sailor's adage, "Brown—run aground; white—you might; green or blue—sail right through." Small green mangrove islands, which appeared to be uninhabited, broke up the flat waterscape. *What a welcome change,* he thought, *from New York*. It appeared to be removed, so remote, so isolated. It looked like he felt; it drew him in. In all his travels, it was like no place he'd ever seen before—or at least ever noticed.

He made his way up to the galley. Happily, the crew had brewed a pot of strong, black coffee, and he poured himself a steaming mugful and went back to his seat, just as the co-pilot turned on the seat belt sign indicating their approach to Marathon.

They were heading south over the Everglades. As the captain banked the plane to the left and then left again for their final approach, the scenery changed. Now William was looking at the beautiful deep dark-blue waters of the Atlantic Ocean. From this height, he could see deserted beaches and small boats tied at the docks or bobbing on their moorings. Shorebirds, seagulls, herons, and pelicans began their daily search for food. The colors were brilliant. Now he could see why so many artists were drawn to the Florida Keys.

Captain Harding greased a perfect landing, and after a short taxi they pulled up to a small building with a sign on the wall that said PARADISE AVIATION–MARATHON JET CENTER. *Jet Center* seemed to be a misnomer, as most of the aircraft there were small, single-engine planes probably used for sightseeing.

William picked up his luggage, such as it was, and thanked the crew as the co-pilot opened the door, which unfolded into a staircase.

"Don't forget your mobile phone, Mr. McKay," Captain Harding said, handing it to him along with a charger. The unwieldy device barely fit into William's pants pocket. He squinted into the bright morning sun as he stepped out of the plane, wishing he had brought sunglasses. The warm air felt great.

An old, dented Ford pickup truck pulled up beside the plane. The driver stepped out and all of a sudden William was standing face-to-face with his father. He looked so different to William now. He seemed shorter and smaller than he'd remembered. Gone was his rigid bearing. He now seemed stoop-shouldered and frail. His brown hair had turned snowy white, made even brighter against his darkly tanned skin. William felt the years of pent-up hatred and rage turning to pity.

The two men faced each other in awkward silence. William didn't offer his hand; nor did his father.

Finally, William said, "Still driving Fords, I see."

The old man chuckled. "We Scottish have to protect our frugal image, you know."

William joined his father in the laugh.

"God, you look awful, kid," Leo said. "What the hell happened to you? And what's with the getup?" Before William could answer, he said, "Never mind, jump in the truck. The tournament starts in an hour and we've got some driving to do. You can tell me later."

William walked around to the passenger side of the truck cab with his dueling pistol case only to find an old mutt in the passenger seat. As he opened the door, the dog glanced up at him, then put his head back down and started moaning. "That's Dorado," his father said, frowning. "He ain't feelin' too good. Maybe ate a snake or a scorpion or something. Do you mind riding back there?" He pointed to the bed of the pickup truck.

"Sure," William said, closing the door, storing his rosewood case, and vaulting over the side of the truck, if only to flaunt the fact to his father that he still had some of his youth and agility. "I love flyin' down highways in the back of a dirty old pickup truck in my tuxedo."

Climbing behind the wheel, his father said, "I didn't say you had to dress for the tournament, you know."

The drive north up the old divided highway was unremarkable, William thought. It could have been a road in any city or town in Florida, lined with fast-food chain restaurants, gas stations, hotels, and retail stores. The vehicles seemed to have an even mix of Florida and out-of-state plates. There were a lot of white or pastel-colored rental cars.

Sitting with his back against the cab of the truck, he tried to get comfortable, but it was impossible. The suspension on this old junker was shot. Every time they hit the smallest bump, he shot straight up in the air and came crashing down hard on a different part of his backside.

Suddenly, fifteen minutes from the Marathon Airport, the scenery changed dramatically for the better. The divided four-lane highway gave way to a paved two-lane road, like a long ribbon separating the shallow waters of the Florida Bay from the deep water of the Atlantic. The fast-food joints were replaced with signs for local joints with names like The Hog's Breath Saloon, Rum Runners, and The Wreck and Galley Grill.

Even in the butt-battering back of the old pickup, William felt himself relaxing. He looked down to see what this ride was doing to what remained of his blood-spattered tailored tux. He shrugged. *I don't think I am going to be invited to any black-tie events anytime soon*, he thought. As his father's truck reached the top of the bridge crossing Channels Two and Five, fifty feet above sea level, his untied necktie blew off in the wind. For the first time he could remember, William felt totally free.

CHAPTER 7

DAY ONE—THE BONEFISH

Soon they were passing a road sign that said, WELCOME TO ISLAMORADA—SPORT-FISHING CAPITAL OF THE WORLD. The tide was out. He saw flocks of white ibis searching the mud for food. On the other side of the road, workmen were putting the final touches to a traveling carnival in a park. Near a bridge called Indian Key, he saw a guy in a small skiff fighting what he would later find out was a large saltwater fish called a tarpon. And everywhere were palm trees gently swaying in the breeze off the ocean. *This must be the capital of this Conch Republic,* he thought.

Passing through a small village, he saw signs for a restaurant named Papa Joe's, The Green Turtle Inn, with an illuminated turtle with a blinking red eye waving his flippers over the name, an upscale resort called the Cheeca Lodge, a grocery store called The Trading Post, and several marinas.

His father slowed his truck and made a left into the driveway of the Lorelei Tiki Bar and Restaurant. Out front was a twenty-foot-tall, thirty-foot-long signboard featuring a topless blond mermaid smiling in repose, a welcoming beacon to wayward sailors, fishermen, and other assorted reprobates. Across the mermaid's fetching middle hung a big banner that said FATHER AND SON CHARITY GRAND SLAM.

The parking lot was a hurricane of activity. Anglers, guides, and tournament officials were scurrying around, seeing to last-minute details. Leo parked, and William jumped down from the bed of the truck. A deeply tanned rough-and-tumble guy, maybe a few years younger than William, swaggered up to the truck to greet Leo.

"Good morning, Leo. You barely made it on time."

"Hi, Cole," his father said.

Cole must be our fishing guide, William thought.

After shaking hands with his father, Cole removed his sunglasses and looked William up and down the way the gang leader in *Rebel Without a Cause* looked at James Dean before their knife fight at the observatory.

Finally Cole spoke. "Leo, what's this?"

"That, Cole, is my son," William's father said calmly.

"What the hell is he wearing?" Cole asked, continuing to speak as if William weren't there.

"I think they're called tuxedos, Cole. They're worn sometimes by civilized gentlemen."

"Is he a secret agent, Leo?" Cole asked, bringing on laughter from the other guides standing nearby.

"Doubtful," William's father answered.

"Well, then, is he retarded?" Cole asked.

The laughter subsided and William felt his fists begin to clench.

Before his father could say anything, a chubby, balding guide with a brace on his wrist across the parking lot yelled over, "Hey, Cole, what's with Mr. Tux? Is he a waiter or your prom date?"

The other guides laughed again.

Cole shouted back, "Hey, Bobby, what's wrong with your wrist? You get that whackin' off between divorces or what?"

Everybody roared, including William, happy to be at least temporarily out of Cole's range of fire.

Just then a flashbulb went off as a short guy in a straw hat took a picture of Cole standing on one side of Leo with William on the other.

"Team name?" he asked William's father.

"McKay, M-C-K- A-Y," he answered.

"Okay. Good luck out there," the little man said, moving on to the next grouping of men.

Leo looked at William, then pointed to the Florida Key Outfitters next to the dock. "Kid, go over there and get some duds. You look like an idiot."

William couldn't argue with that. As he turned and walked toward the shop, he overheard his father say to Cole, "C'mere, kid. I want to talk to you." *Maybe he's going to tell him to behave,* William thought.

The Outfitters was a far cry from the old tackle shop in Saranac Lake that William's grandfather had often taken him to visit as a boy in the Adirondacks. Instead of dark and musty, this shop was bright and air-conditioned. Bait tanks were replaced with islands of colorful flies and attractive fishing clothing with lightweight shirts in pastel colors . . . aqua blues and greens and coral colors that an old-timer in upper New York State wouldn't have been seen dead in.

Large rod racks held rows of tall, elegant, tapered fly-fishing rods instead of the spinning rods and bait casters of William's youth.

The walls were painted white, instead of stained wood, but still served as the background to a variety of pictures of men and women standing in boats or wading shallow water, showing off their prize catches. Gone, however, were the dockside pictures of fishermen posing with their day's catch of twenty-five dead fish. William knew that in today's world, *catch and release* was replacing the old adage of *catch 'em and cook 'em.*

Written with an artist's touch, over a rack of men's clothing, William read the words:

THE CHARM OF FISHING IS THAT IT IS THE PURSUIT OF WHAT IS ELUSIVE BUT ATTAINABLE, A PERPETUAL SERIES OF OCCASIONS FOR HOPE.

—JOHN BUCHAN

Yeah right, William thought to himself as he gathered up an armful of fishing shorts and shirts. *I hope that I'll find some charm in this three-day fishing tournament.*

Next, he walked over to the revolving countertop carousel to check out sunglasses. A woman's voice from behind him said, "If you're fishing, you should get polarized lenses so you can see through the water."

He turned to look at her. She was stunning. She looked to be in her mid-twenties, about five foot eight, dark-brown hair cut short, a bronze tan, a slender figure, and a beautiful smile. Her wide brown eyes were the darkest he'd ever seen.

"Can you show me?" he managed to say.

She spun the carousel and picked out a pair with amber-tinted lenses, then slipped them on his face. He noticed her long manicured fingers.

"Nice," she said.

"Handsome?" he asked.

"No, just nice," she said, smiling.

"Do you charge a consulting fee?" William asked, and she smiled again.

"That's a pretty nasty cut on your forehead. It could use a stitch or two," she said.

From outside, a voice on the loudspeaker said, "Anglers and guides to your boats! The blessing of the fleet will begin in five minutes."

"Gotta go," she said, turning for the door. "By the way, the tux? Handsome."

William bolted for the changing room, deciding that he would not throw the tux away as he'd planned. He scrambled into some of his new togs, transferred his clunky mobile phone into a pocket of his shorts, and put everything else in a bag that he'd pick up when they returned to the dock.

Heading outside toward Cole's slip where his skiff was docked, William noticed a wooden sign with a carved quotation posted by the boardwalk.

THE GODS DO NOT DEDUCT FROM MAN'S ALLOTTED SPAN THE HOURS SPENT IN FISHING.

Man, William thought, *folks down here really love their fishing quotes.*

He looked up to see Cole approaching with two old cardboard boxes of fish guts, dripping a line of slime as he went.

"Cole, do you know—?"

It's a Babylonian proverb," he answered. "I put it there myself."

"Hey listen, Cole," William said, "maybe we got off on the wrong foot before." He extended his hand. "I'm Will McKay."

Cole shoved the open boxes of chum into his hands. Stinky goo started dripping down William's new clothes.

"I know who you are," Cole said. "Now pitch those and get in the skiff."

His father was already on board, spreading suntan lotion on his arms. "Here you are, son," he said, handing William the tube. "It's gonna be a hot one today. Our fly rods are stowed under the gunnels, and our lunches and drinks are in the ice chest. I've got lots of water, iced tea, Cokes, and a few beers for the ride in."

Cole came back to the boat, finishing a cigarette that he butted in a designated can of sand on the dock, untied the line, stepped to the center console between William and his father, and fired up the engine.

As they motored out to join about eighty other boats collecting in Lorelei's little harbor, William looked around Cole's skiff, which was spotlessly clean. What he lacked in manners, William thought, he apparently made up for in good housekeeping. Otherwise, it was about identical to the others. Seventeen and a half feet long, it was made of fiberglass and had a bench seat amidships behind the console for the two anglers and captain. Immediately in front of the console was an ice chest with a padded top, no doubt for a third angler if there was one on a chartered trip. The bow of the boat offered a large, smooth platform for the anglers to stand on. A stainless-steel platform was built over the rear-mounted outboard so the guide could look for fish as he propelled the boat around the flats with the eighteen-foot fiberglass push pole that for now was fastened to the top of one of the gunnels.

In the center of the now crowded harbor, Cole cut the engine and drifted among the fleet of boats, each with a captain and two anglers. The sun had risen well above the bordering palm trees that swayed gently in the northeasterly wind. Congenial insults bounced back and forth among fellow competitors, most of whom seemed to know one another pretty well, or well enough to belittle one another's skills, chances of winning, and occasionally their heritage and aberrant sex life or lack thereof. Some of the stuff was directed at William's dad, who had obviously become a well-accepted member of this community of anglers.

Suddenly, an air horn went off, silencing the chatter and drawing everyone's attention to a busty redhead, probably in her fifties, standing on the dock, a microphone in her hands.

"Who's that?" William asked his father.

"That's Mrs. Reno."

William couldn't help but notice the smile that crossed his father's lips. "She's our mayor and magistrate. She also owns the most popular gin mill in town."

"She also gives your old man an occasional knob wash," Cole chimed in.

"That's enough of that, Captain." Leo seemed to blush.

"Good morning, everyone," Mrs. Reno boomed. "Welcome to the first annual Islamorada Father and Son Charity Grand Slam Fly-Fishing Tournament!"

A huge cheer went up from the assembled anglers.

"Here are the rules," she said, "Rule one is to have three days of fun." More cheers from the crowd. "Rule two, only fly rods, no bait." The anglers quieted. This was the serious part. "Rule three, your target species are bonefish, tarpon, and permit. Rule four, first team to catch one of each wins the tournament. But remember, each angler has to catch at least one of the three. Rule five, International Game Fish Association rules apply and no leader can exceed fifteen feet."

"What's a leader?" William asked his father.

"That's the monofilament line we connect to the end of the fly line," he said.

Mrs. Reno continued, "Regardless of when any boat releases all three species, fishing goes on for three days. Cast at every species you see and photograph your catches before you release them. Please photograph tarpon in the water. This is a catch-and-release tournament and we want to see all of our caught fish live to fight another day.

"And again, have some fun out there and do some father–son bonding. Here are some icebreakers: Fathers, ask your sons if they've ever gotten lucky. Sons, ask your fathers if they've ever smoked a joint, but remember that they'll probably lie. Lying is what all fishermen do best!"

The crowd roared with laughter.

"Finally, and seriously, all of your entry fees are going to the Cystic Fibrosis Foundation for research to find a cure for that dreaded childhood disease, so thank you all very much. Now everyone shut up for the blessing of the fleet."

Silence fell over the fleet of skiffs. Some of the participants took off their hats, some stood, and some bowed their heads.

"Great God and Father of all fishermen," Mrs. Reno began, "we ask for your blessing on this fleet. Keep our captains patient and our anglers humble, the beer cold and the fishing hot, and more than anything else, give us this time to enjoy the beauty of Your creation and to also remember why we are here . . . to help find a cure that will save the lives of our most priceless catch, our precious children. Please bless this fleet and bring them all back safely before sundown. Amen."

Amens were murmured from the boats.

"Lines in whenever you wish, but out of the water by three thirty p.m. So without further ado, gentlemen, start your engines!"

Eighty outboard motors sprang to life.

"Now I need a starter's pistol," Mrs. Reno shouted. "Anybody out there have a gun? No, forget I asked that."

Everyone laughed. (William had left his locked in his father's truck.)

"On my voice then, take your mark . . . get set . . . go fishing!"

Almost as one, the skiffs turned toward the hundred-yard channel that led to the Florida Bay. The captains were not allowed to give their engines full thrust as the harbor and channel were no-wake zones, but there was a lot of jockeying for position and a renewal of jokes and curses.

William stood up in front of his seat to get a better look at the fleet. When they got to the end of the channel, Cole turned his baseball cap around and said to William, "Hey, waiter, you better hold on."

"What?" William asked just as Cole jammed the throttle forward.

The nose of the skiff shot up in the air and William got knocked back to his seat, barely able to grab hold of the stern poling platform to keep from falling out the back.

The nose of the boat came down as the skiff planed out then jumped ahead as if it had been shot out of a cannon. The resulting rush of wind caught the bill of William's new hat and blew it off his head into the waters of the Florida Bay. *Guess I'll just fish hatless today*, he thought.

At first the skiffs were packed in tight, creating a sea of turbulence with their wakes. Then the fleet thinned out as the captains headed off in different directions, racing to get to their favorite fishing spot on the rising tide.

Cole's skiff literally flew over the shallow aquamarine water at fifty miles an hour. They were heading due south, hugging the markers on the right side of a wide channel. They'd completely broken away from the pack when Cole threw the boat into a steep sliding right-hand turn to the west and into the beautiful Florida Bay that William had flown over just a few hours earlier.

They ran in silence for about twenty minutes, skimming over the shallow, calm waters with the rising sun on their backs. Their charging boat startled meandering fish and resting seabirds. William was consumed with the beauty of the place. He felt a million miles away from the mean streets of New York, the cold, the treachery, the banquet, the scene, the embarrassment, the gunshot, the lost love. They all seemed to dissolve now in the wake of the speeding skiff.

They ran for another five minutes or so until Cole pulled back the throttle, turned his hat around, wiped his sunglasses with the red bandanna he wore around his neck, and stood up to scan the water.

Cole unfastened the push pole and put one end in the mud as he climbed up on the poling platform for a better 360-degree look around the boat.

Leo said, "Whatcha got, Cole?"

Cole pointed toward the horizon directly in front of the skiff, "Pelicans diving pilchards at twelve o'clock." He turned ninety degrees right. "Dolphins rounding up mullet at three o'clock." Cole turned again and looked at William. "An ignorant rookie who doesn't know his ass from a hole in the ground at six o'clock."

Leo tried to suppress a chuckle and failed.

Cole turned right again. "And a couple of big pushes up on that long bank at nine o'clock."

"What's he mean, Dad," William asked his father, "about three out of four of those things?"

"You don't know nothing, do you, waiter?" Cole said.

"Quit it, you two," Leo barked.

"We lay the boat out like a clock, William, with the bow being twelve o'clock. That makes it easier to point out fish," his father explained. "Big fish drive small baits like pilchards to the surface and birds dive on them for something to eat. That was twelve o'clock. Porpoise school up larger baitfish like mullet, then take turns eating them. That's what he saw at three o'clock. Six o'clock you know, and at nine o'clock directly to our left, bonefish push up onto the shallow flats to find crabs and other crustaceans, and my guess is that's where we're headed."

"Right on, Leo," Cole said. "Grab that eight-weight rod with the small crab pattern fly on it and let out some line."

Leo did as he was told and turned to William. "You ever cast a fly before, son?"

"Once," he said. "For a few hours on a business trip, I went fishing with the governor of Montana and—"

"Oh God," he heard Cole say.

"So I'll take that as a no," his father said.

Cole chuckled.

"Okay," his dad said, "see that cooler over there? Sit on it."

Leo walked up to the bow of the boat with the fly rod as Cole held the boat steady with the end of the pole. The old man reached into his pocket for a handful of change and tossed it into the water.

"What was that for?" William asked.

"Nothing in life is free, kid," Leo said. "You gotta pay the fish."

Leo unhooked the little brown crab fly and pulled about fifteen yards of fly line off the reel.

"Fly fishing is made up of three parts," Leo said. "Presentation or casting; retrieval or stripping; and then catching. If you don't get the first and second right, you won't do much of the third.

"First, on presentation, unlike the governor of Montana's stocked trout stream, we have to cast long distances in saltwater, sometimes eighty, ninety, a hundred feet, often into the wind. Where we land the fly is important. We want to land it in front of the fish so that we can draw it through his field of vision. We never want to land it too close to the fish unless the water is muddy or it will spook him. Behind him, he won't see it, and if you hit him with the fly, he'll bolt."

Leo began moving his right arm back and forth in a series of casting motions. "You use your entire arm, as opposed to just your wrist, to create a loop in the air with your line. Once you've formed a good loop, the weight will pull itself out. Then you pick your target and let it go." He stopped his graceful forward motion and let the fly land about fifty feet from the boat.

"Now that you have your distance and have made a good presentation, point your rod tip down," Leo said, "and you are ready to work on your retrieval.

"The flies we use are all designed and tied to look like food that saltwater fish like to eat—minnows, small eels, worms, or crustaceans, like the crab pattern we're using this morning. All these critters have two things in common. They never move toward a predator . . . always away . . . and none of them stay still for long when they sense danger.

"The point of the retrieval is to make the fly look to the fish like its real-life counterpart. Unlike other kinds of fishing, we don't retrieve line with our reel, but with our free hand. This is called stripping in line and gives us the chance to vary our speed, length, and rhythm to try and fool the fish. A long strip makes a minnow fly appear to be swimming, while a choppy strip with small delays makes a crab fly appear to be jumping."

"What do I need to know about number three—catching?" William asked.

"If you don't do number one and number two right, you won't get a chance to do number three. Also, catching is all about concentration, not how strong you are. Good catchers are the best concentrators. Relax your mind or lose your concentration, and you'll lose your fish every time."

Leo handed William the rod. "Now you try some casts."

Totally out of his element, William made a terrible mess of his first try.

"That's not what I did at all. Go again," Leo said.

On the next try, William formed a loop but lost his rhythm and watched as the fly line dropped limply in the water next to the boat.

"Use your arm, not just your wrist," Leo said. "Don't hold your breath. Third time's a charm."

He was right. William used his arm, slowed down, and managed to get all of the fly line in the air before letting the crab fly land softly in the water.

From the platform Cole called down, "Two bonefish at twelve o'clock, fifty feet moving right to left."

Leo said, "Intercept them, throw toward ten o'clock."

William tried. The fly landed at approximately seven o'clock.

"Jeez," his father whispered, "can't you tell time? That's not even close."

Cole said, "That's okay, they're turning. Put your rod tip down and strip in line as fast as you can till I say stop."

William stripped line in until Cole whispered, "Stop . . . bump it. If you feel him bite, don't lift the rod, just keep on stripping till he pulls line out of your hand."

As he bumped the line, he watched a silvery shadow of a fish stick its tail up and pounce down on the fly. The line grew tight and then started flying off the reel and out of the boat fast.

"I've got one," William said, giving his companions a glimpse of the glaringly obvious.

Suddenly, his mobile phone rang and William dug it out of his shorts pocket and put it to his ear. "Hello?

"Lionel," William said to Lionel Johnson from his public relations department. "Yes, I'm out of town. They want a comment before they go to press? Well, tell them—"

Plink. He felt a stab at the other end of the fishing line, then everything went limp.

Cole jumped down from the poling platform and grabbed the mobile phone from William and threw it as far as he could into the ocean.

William looked at him as if he'd gone mad. "What the hell are you doing?"

"You can do one thing or the other, but you can't do both. Not on my boat."

William looked him in the eye and said, "That was an important call."

Cole said, "That was an important fish."

After a moment of deadlock, Leo shooed Cole back to the stern of the boat and said to William, "Bad form, kid. You flunked concentration, so you're benched. Sit your ass down on the cooler."

William knew that they were both right. As Leo stepped to the bow, William settled in on the cooler top and looked around. Big sharks swam past stingrays burrowing in the mud. Cole poled them by a bunch of barracuda that lay still until they were frightened by the boat and swam away. They poled past a mangrove island and startled a flock of resting roseate spoonbills, a spectacular mass of pink and white against a cloudless blue sky. Last time he'd seen spoonbills was on the rivers of Vietnam.

The windless day made it easier for the fish to see the boat coming. Cole put them near a lot of fish, but many spooked the minute Leo started casting. Several others just ignored their fly.

Leo cast well, but when he occasionally messed up, he wasn't exempt from Cole's jibes. On one flat, he threw at a large tailing bonefish and the fly hit her right in the tail, scaring her away.

"Goddamn it, Leo," Cole shouted, "they don't eat with their asses!"

Every so often, Cole jumped down from the platform, fired up the engine, and ran for a while before positioning them on another flat in search of their target species. The rushing wind was a welcome break from the searing heat of the burning sun.

As the sun rose toward midday, William relaxed. He looked at his watch. It was 12:05 p.m. "Hey, you guys getting hungry?"

His father said yes and Cole just grunted.

He opened a bag full of sandwiches marked TURKEY, HAM AND CHEESE, and ROAST BEEF.

Cole said, "I'll have ham and cheese, waiter, with a little mustard and no mayo."

He tried to open one of the little packets of mustard and it squirted right on the crotch of his new shorts.

"Nice play, Shakespeare," Cole quipped, "but I'd rather have it on the sandwich. You'll never get to be headwaiter that way."

William opened another packet, got the contents on the sandwich, wrapped it in a napkin, and started to hand it to Cole.

"Hold on," Cole said, looking back over his shoulder at Leo. "I've got a big single quartering toward us, left to right at seven o'clock, a hundred feet."

Putting the sandwich back in the bag, William resumed his perch to watch the action.

Leo swung around and pointed the rod toward where he thought he saw the bonefish.

"That's him," Cole said. "When he's in your range, give him a three-foot lead and let it sink."

William's father waited about ten seconds and made a perfect cast. He didn't have to wait after that. The bonefish grabbed the fly before it hit the bottom, felt the sting of the barbless hook, and took off.

The old angler slowly lifted his rod tip, putting a good bend in the rod and letting the fish go where it wanted to go, which was straight away from the boat at a high rate of speed. The reel whirred as the line flew off. On and on the bonefish went, not showing any signs of tiring. Then, about 250 yards from the boat, it stopped, giving Leo a chance to start reeling it in. He lifted up and reeled down, all the time keeping the line tight.

"Good pressure, Leo," Cole shouted. "Try and lead him away from those two mangrove shoots. He gets you tangled on one of those, he'll break you off."

The fish took off again but without the same energy as before, then turned.

"He's getting tired now," Cole said, sticking one end of the pole into the mud and tying the line attached to his platform to the other end. Once the boat was staked up, he jumped down and pulled out a large net from one of the hatches.

"Bring him straight in, Leo. There are a couple of hungry-looking lemon sharks nosing around."

William's dad brought the fish to the boat, and Cole netted him out of the water on the first try.

"Yes!" his dad said.

"What do we do with him now?" William asked.

"We measure and photograph him. He's got to be at least eighteen inches. Then we release him as fast as we can. No sense killin' 'em; they're not good eating anyway."

Cole laid the fish down on a yardstick while Leo photographed him.

"Twenty-one inches, Leo. We've got our bonefish," Cole said, smiling. Cole took the fly out of the fish's little mouth, gently put it back in the water, held it by the tail, and moved it back and forth a few times, all the while watching for the sharks. The fish hovered for a few minutes, then with a sudden burst pulled away from Cole's light grip, quickly disappearing into the brackish water.

"Well done, Leo," Cole said as he washed the slime off his hands. He stood up and gave the old man a handshake and a big hug.

"Thanks, Cole," Leo said. "Let's have something to eat."

Cole looked William's way. "What's for lunch again, waiter?"

The two fishermen talked about their catch and the next target over their sandwiches, all but ignoring William. After lunch, they started again. The afternoon was a lot like the morning. Leo had a few more shots at fish but came up empty. They put William back on the bow for a few chances, which he blew badly. One time he let the fly go too early, watching it sail into a mangrove island behind them. Another, the fly caught the back of his shirt.

At 3:30 p.m. Cole announced, "Lines out," and they headed for home.

"Kind of a slow day," his father said, but at least they were on the board.

The ride home was beautiful with the afternoon sun at their backs. There was little conversation. Cole maneuvered into his assigned slip at Lorelei, where they were greeted by Dorado, wagging his tail. You could tell by the way the old dog walked around, receiving greetings from the regulars, that he was a real fixture at the marina. They stepped onto the dock.

Leo said, "Thanks, Cole, see you tomorrow at eight."

"Bring that twelve-weight tarpon rod of yours," Cole said.

William said good-bye to Cole, but he either didn't hear him or chose to ignore him.

William stopped at the Outfitters to pick up his clothes. Walking back to the parking lot, he watched his father helping Dorado climb into the truck. The dog managed to get his big paws up on the tailgate, and Leo lifted his rear end up till Dorado could kind of limp into the bed, then flop down for the ride. *Hell to get old*, William thought.

CHAPTER 8

THE CONCH HOUSE

Leo, William, and Dorado chugged north up Islamorada's one main road, US A1A, which was called simply "the highway" by the natives. On the way to his father's house, William spotted a drugstore.

"Would you mind stopping for a minute so I can pick up some toiletries?"

Leo came in, too, and picked up a *Florida Keys Keynoter*. William was glad they didn't have any New York newspapers.

About five miles up the road, his father turned left onto an old oak-lined street called Pippin and then made another left and pulled into the driveway of a small rectangular one-story cottage with a broad front porch that ran the length of the house. The little place looked like it had been uprooted from the Bahamas.

William grabbed his stuff and followed his father up the porch and into the front door. Dorado walked behind him, looking a little unhappy that an interloper was entering his domain.

Inside, Leo said, "Welcome to my humble abode. It's got a living room, kitchen, dining room, john, and two bedrooms, one of which I made into a tackle room. My couch in the living room is old but comfortable. After dinner, I'll make it up for you to sleep on. Why don't you shower up while I make us some dinner? I've got some fresh yellowtail snapper that I can put on the grill."

"Sounds good," William said. After a long day on the water, he was starving.

He stowed his rosewood box under the old couch and took his toiletries and a change of clothes into the bathroom to get cleaned up.

The bathroom looked more like a fishing hall of fame. Every wall was covered with framed fishing photos, most of them featuring his dad and some other guy holding up a huge fish. In most of the pictures, the other guy was Cole. William found himself strangely jealous of Cole for all the time he'd gotten to spend with this man who had walked out of his life so many years ago.

Showered and shaved, he felt human again. After inspecting the wound on his forehead, he dressed and walked into the kitchen, where his father was grilling the yellowtail. Dorado walked over to sniff his crotch.

"The fish smells great, Dad," he said. "Almost covers up the smell of your dog."

"It's you that's doing it to him," his father said. "You're in his space and you make him nervous."

"You don't want to put him out on the porch while we eat?" William asked.

"Naw, it's his house, too. He's got his old bed in my bedroom and he's comfortable," his father said, rubbing his arm. "Let's eat."

They walked into the dining room and sat down at Leo's weathered table, which had two place settings, a bowl with fresh corn on the cob, some french fries on a plate, a salad, and a basket of rolls. His father brought the platter of fish filleted into small strips with lemon wedges on the side. William had a flashback to growing up, remembering that on those rare occasions when he'd had time, his father had loved to grill.

Leo sat down across the table from his son, and with no ceremony they filled their plates and began to eat.

Everything was delicious. There were so many things to say but it was as if neither of them knew where to start, so they made small talk. William asked his father about the derivation of the term *conch*.

"After the Calusa Indians inhabited the Keys, it was later occupied by a group of Americans during the Revolutionary War," Leo explained. "They were British loyalists who did not want to fight against their homeland. They gathered their families and migrated to the Bahamas and here, to the Florida Keys. They were called conchs for their custom of withdrawing into themselves like conchs, paying little or no attention to the outside world."

"Those are the shells people hold to their ear to hear the ocean, right?"

Leo rolled his eyes.

Over dessert, two scoops of vanilla ice cream with chocolate sauce and rich, roasted black coffee, Leo continued with the history lesson about the Keys.

"Completion of the Overseas Highway connecting the islands in 1938 made the Keys much more accessible. People flocked here from the North to enjoy the warm weather and laid-back lifestyle.

"The fishing is fabulous, but the area also attracted writers, artists, poets, and other people interested in a Bohemian lifestyle. Ernest Hemingway, Tennessee Williams, Jack Kerouac, and John Audubon came and did some of their best work here. Land's-end mentality played a big role as well."

"Land's-end mentality," William asked, "what's that mean?"

"Well," Leo continued, "many people over the years have sought refuge here as a place to get away to, an escape from somewhere or someone else. A last resort, a place where no one cares who you are or what you've done. No one here asks any questions. Live and let live is the rule. I guess you could say that the way of the conch is still a time-honored tradition here."

Leo stopped there and seemed to stare off into the distance in silence.

Feeling that this was, perhaps, a prelude to the story that he had come to the Keys to hear, William tried to restart the conversation and asked his father, "Are you now a conch, then?"

"Yeah, I guess I am," Leo said. "A freshwater conch, which is what you become after being here more than seven years." Leo pushed himself gingerly out of his chair. "Listen, kid, I'm not feeling so great. Think I'll go sit on the porch and get some fresh air."

"You okay, Dad?" William asked.

"Yeah, just a little tired," he said. "Would you mind clearing the table?"

"I still have a lot of things on my mind that I think we need to talk about."

"I know, son, we will, I promise," Leo said. "But not tonight, okay?"

His dad and Dorado walked outside, and William cleared the dishes. He looked for a dishwasher to stack them in and, finding none, decided to wash and dry them by hand. It was a tiny kitchen and finding a place to put everything away was easy, so he did that as well.

William walked out on the porch to find his dad smoking a cigarette, listening to a New York Rangers hockey game on a transistor radio, and once again rubbing his arm, old Dorado curled up at his feet.

"Your arm all right?" he asked him.

"Yeah, it's fine," he said. "I think I must have strained it the other day when Cole and I were pulling traps."

"Crab traps?" he asked.

"Yeah," he said. "Every resident down here is allowed to put out five stone crab traps. Cole and I pull them every Thursday evening, rip off one claw on each if it's big enough, and release the crab. Doesn't hurt 'em and in a couple of months it grows right back. It's like pickin' apples on a tree, and the boiled legs are delicious. Cole and I have a bet to see who catches more by the end of the season."

"So, this Cole guy," William asked, "is he your best friend or something? I mean, what's up with him?"

"What do you mean?" his father asked.

"Why is he such an asshole?"

His dad chuckled and looked away off into the distance. "He's got his own reasons."

"I don't get it, Dad," William said to him, reaching over and turning down his radio. "Why do you do this?"

"Do what?" he asked.

"Live like this," he said. "Down here in this shack? What are you trying to prove? I know damn well you left the company with plenty of money."

"Proving things is a young man's game, William. I'm seventy-five years old. I just want to fish."

"Fish?"

"Yeah, fish. Is that so hard to understand?" he asked, looking at his son.

"There are more important things in life than fishing, Dad."

"That's right, son, there are," he answered, "but I've pissed most of those things away."

William started to say something but thought better of it. His dad snubbed out his cigarette in a sand-filled coffee can and said, "Listen, son, I'm shitcanned. I'm gonna shower and turn in now. Big day tomorrow. We're going after our tarpon."

"Okay," he said, "you got anything to drink around here?"

"My doc says I gotta take it easy on booze now, William," he said, "so I keep the house dry. There's a bar about a mile up the road on the left, Mrs. Reno's place behind Marker 88 restaurant."

"Can I borrow your truck?" William asked as they both stood up.

"No."

"No?"

"You're gonna be drinking, right?" he asked. "What kind of a father would I be if I let you drink and drive? And besides, that truck's a classic."

"Dad, I'm—"

"Walking," he said, making a little walking motion with two fingers.

"Okay, Dad," he said, "I'll see you tomorrow. You sure you're all right?"

"If I were any better, I'd cancel my life insurance."

Now William knew where he'd gotten that expression from.

CHAPTER 9

MRS. RENO'S

William walked out the door and down the quiet street toward the highway. The full moon was rising and lit the way as tree frogs and crickets chirped away. An occasional dove cooed by the side of the road. A startled blue heron took wing and flew off squawking into the gentle breeze. Traffic was light on the highway. He walked past Lookout Lodge Resort and turned left at a neon sign that said MRS. RENO'S CONCH BAR and underneath it WELCOME ANGLERS. Crossing a car-filled parking lot, he followed a green neon arrow that pointed down a wooden plank pathway through dark mangrove woods. Multicolored tiki lights were strung on trees along the winding trail. As he came to a clearing, he could hear music in the distance.

The path opened up to a gorgeous moonlit beach and a rustic, thatch-roofed, fresh-air beach bar, filled to capacity.

On the far side of the property there was a free-standing bandstand in front of a dance floor. Large and small tables were scattered around, and those closest

to the bar and dance floor were packed with revelers. A banner that stretched between two palm trees read OPEN-MIKE NIGHT.

The place was filled with suntanned locals and sunburned tourists. They were all gathered around holding drink glasses and laughing as a shirtless guy stood at the mike caterwauling some tune or another. As William got closer, he could see it was Bobby, the mouthy fishing guide, who was gripping his cocktail in the hand supported by the wrist brace with the microphone stand in the other. His upper arms bore what looked like naval service tattoos, and on his chest was a large inked tarpon, which seemed to be leaping out of his pants up to his hairy chest. It wasn't a pretty sight.

The three-piece house band winced as a red-faced Bobby belted his way through an off-key, throaty rendition of Jimmy Buffett's "Why Don't We Get Drunk and Screw?"

When he finished, he kissed his biceps, grabbed his crotch, then pumped his fist in the air. He yelled into the microphone, "Parrot Heads Rule," extending his thumb and pinkie and shaking his hand in a hang-loose salute. The crowd cheered and applauded as an embarrassed woman, who must have been Bobby's wife, tried to coax him down from the stage.

There was one seat left at the bar, so William sat down. Mrs. Reno, standing behind the bar drying a glass, looked up at him and said, "Holy shit."

"Yes, Mrs. Reno," he said, "but some of my friends call me William."

"I know who you are, sugar," she said. "You're Leo McKay's boy. He brags about you all the time. I was just a little surprised to see you here—that's all. What can I get for you?"

William pointed at Bobby on the stage and said, "What's he having?"

"He's been drinking Rum Gaffs, one of my special concoctions."

"Bring it on," he said.

"Sure, honey." She smiled. "You want a Bloody-Gaff or a Kill-Gaff?"

"A Kill-Gaff, please."

"Thatta boy," she said.

As Mrs. Reno turned to make his drink, an enchanting woman's voice cut through the noisy crowd, hushing them to silence. William turned to the stage to see that the voice belonged to the beautiful girl from the Outfitters who'd helped him pick out his sunglasses, now coincidentally singing the very last song he'd heard before leaving New York. She was standing at the microphone wearing a sundress and looking even more beautiful than he had remembered. She was magnetic.

He swallowed hard and listened. Her lips were close to the mike, and she sang in a tender whispery voice:

Unforgettable, that's what you are
Unforgettable, though near or far

A few couples got up to snuggle on the dance floor. As the band's guitarist did a jazzy solo, the girl closed her eyes and swayed to the music. William was totally captivated. She started to sing again.

Unforgettable in every way
And forever more, that's how you'll stay

She finished the song and the crowd erupted into wild applause, shouts and whistles. William just sat at the bar and stared at her. Mrs. Reno came back and set his drink on the bar in front of him and said, "You know her, darlin'?"

"Who?"

"The little sweetie on the stage," she answered.

"We've met," he said. "But I'd like to get to know her better."

"Well, you better hurry, William," Mrs. Reno said. "She's only in town for a few days."

"What's her name?" he asked.

"Jenny Hunter. Looks like she's heading this way. You wanna buy her a drink?"

"I wanna buy her a house," he said.

"Better start with a drink."

"Great, could you make one, please?" he asked.

"Already have," she laughed, putting in front of him a slender, delicate glass filled with chilled orange juice and champagne.

As Jenny approached, William picked up the drinks and stood to greet her. "That was great," he stammered. "Can I buy you a drink?"

"Thanks," she said. "It looks like you already have."

He laughed. "Here, take my seat."

"Thanks," she said again, "but I'd rather sit with you at a table."

As he paid the bill, the band took a break. They walked over to a small table away from the rest of the crowd. They sat down, and he put her drink in front of her.

"I'm Will," he said.

"Jenny," she answered. "Nice to meet you."

"Well, cheers." They touched glasses. "You have a beautiful voice," he told her.

"Thanks," she said. "I wish I could remember the lyrics of more songs, but they seem to go in and out of my head. Speaking of heads, didn't I tell you to take care of that cut on your forehead?"

"Yes, you did."

"Why didn't you do it, then?" she asked.

"I was hoping I'd run into you again, and it would give us something to talk about."

Jenny laughed and said, "Let me see it."

William leaned forward so she could examine the wound. The touch of her hand was gentle and cool on his sunburned forehead.

"You are a mess," she said.

"Tell me about it."

"Come on, let's go to my car," she said.

He wasn't sure why they were going to her car, but he was positive that he would have followed her anywhere.

They walked down the path together through the parking lot toward a rental Jeep.

She opened the back and pointed for him to sit on the tailgate, then reached into the trunk and pulled out an old-fashioned black leather doctor's case. The Jeep was loaded with gear and a fly-rod case.

Jenny cleaned the cut on his forehead with some clear alcohol on a white gauze pad. It stung but he clenched his teeth. He didn't want to start with this beautiful woman by appearing to be a baby.

"It's too late to stitch this," she said. "You're going to have to let it heal from the inside out."

"You're a doctor?"

"I am," she said, smiling, "and the daughter of a doctor as well. That's where I got this old medical case."

"Will I have a scar, Doc?" he asked.

"A pretty big one." She leaned closer and spread some cooling salve over the wound.

As she worked, he couldn't take his eyes off her—her hair, her neck, her eyes, her lips—as she spoke.

"You've also got a bad sunburn, Will," she said. "I've got some aloe lotion. That'll help." She opened a jar and spread some on his face. Her touch was magical.

"I'm going to put a bandage on that wound. Keep it on for a day or so, and then leave it uncovered so it can get some air, but don't go swimming for a few days. Try to keep it clean and I'll give you this salve to put on it at least four times a day. It will speed up the healing," she said. "It's a nasty wound. How did you get it?"

"A minor misjudgment," William said.

"Looks like there's a little gunpowder around the cut," she said, pausing and looking into his eyes. "Listen, Will, I've seen too much anger in my life and I want you to know that there is absolutely nothing I detest more than violence."

"Jenny, I'm a peaceful man. Not always at peace, but peaceful."

"Uh-huh," she said, not totally able to contain a small smile.

"Do you fish?" he asked her, looking at her fly-rod case as she put her doctor's bag away.

"A little," she said, "but I've got a lot to learn."

"How about I buy you some dinner so I can properly repay you for your services?"

"Thanks, but I've already eaten," she said.

"So have I," he said, blushing a little as she smiled again. "How 'bout I win you a stuffed animal then?"

"Huh?"

"C'mon, let's take a ride. I'm carless tonight. Mind if we take your Jeep?"

"No problem," she said, "as long as you drive," and handed him the keys.

"Ah, an old-fashioned girl."

"Only sometimes," she said, laughing.

CHAPTER 10

THE TURTLE

"So you're just passing through?" William asked as he drove.

"I'm starting up a new clinic in Alice Town in a few days."

"Where's that?"

"Bimini. It's a small island in the Bahamas."

"And where are you coming from?" he asked.

"Bad-marriageville," she told him.

"I've driven through there once myself."

They both laughed.

"So what happened?"

"It's kind of a long story," she said. "I'm from a little town in Wisconsin called Appleton. After college at Madison, I went to med school at the university and met Rick, the star running back. Second-team All-American—got drafted by the Green Bay Packers.

"We got married right after his graduation. It was going to be a great life; we were going to move to Green Bay, where he would play football and I would practice medicine."

"And?"

She glanced out the passenger-side window. "The dream went wrong. Rick blew out his knee in training camp and the Packers let him go. He tried a few jobs but couldn't get used to life without adulation. The harder I worked to advance my medical career, the more morose he became.

"Then he started drinking heavily and lying around at home. I came home late one night from my rounds at the hospital and he was drunk. He accused me of having an affair with one of the other interns. He wouldn't let up; he shoved me into a corner of the living room. Then he hit me."

"What'd you do?" William asked her.

"I left," she said. "I told him I'd be back for my things later, got in my car, and left with him cursing me all the way out of the driveway. I drove to Appleton and asked my dad if I could have my room back."

"Would you ever go back with him," William asked, "if he got his life back together?"

"No way," she said. "I called an attorney friend of my dad's the next day and got a restraining order against him and filed for a divorce. My lawyer instructed me to stay in Wisconsin for a year so that I couldn't be charged with abandonment. I worked hard and put in an application for a job at the new clinic in Bimini. The year was up last Monday, I got my divorce decree on Tuesday, and, as they say in the song, I hit the road, Jack, and here I am."

"I'm glad you're okay," William said.

"How about your life, Will? Some ex reach a bad conclusion about you?"

"Pretty much," he said. "As far as women are concerned, I think the book on me is that I'm a good date and a bad husband. Looking back, I can't blame my ex. With my dad leaving, my mother getting sick, and my needs to take care of her and to prove myself, I became absolutely driven. I was never around for my wife. There was no shouting or fighting; our marriage just ended. I actually liked the security of being married. I was even on my way for another try till I caught my fiancée doing the wild thing with one of the young guys who worked for me. I ended up leaving town in a hurry."

"That rapid departure have something to do with that gunshot wound on your forehead?"

"You'd win that bet and I'll pay it up with a Ferris wheel ride," William said as they pulled up to the little carnival that he'd seen them setting up that morning.

"I'm a fool for Ferris wheels," she said, getting out of the car, flashing that great smile again.

It wasn't that high, but from the top the view of the moonlit waters of the Florida Bay was breathtaking. The seats were small, forcing them to sit close. He held Jenny's hand and she didn't take it away.

After the ride, William and Jenny walked down the small midway, still holding hands. They walked past kids and their folks shooting BB guns or throwing darts at balloons to win prizes, lining up for cotton candy and funnel cakes. The background music was supplied by an old calliope.

At the end of the midway was a booth with an aluminum pond filled with small, carved wooden fish. The object was to use a small wooden fishing rod with a string and a large, dull hook attached to snag one of the fish and win a prize.

"Let's try it," William said, and paid a dollar to the Asian granny who was overseeing the game.

She handed them a small rod and said, "Good luck, you catch a winner."

Jenny and William picked out which wooden fish they wanted to go after. Both holding the tiny rod, they began laughing as they tried to slip their hook through the little eyelet on the fish's nose. William noticed that his co-angler had a steady hand, and they hooked their target fish on the second try.

Together they pulled it out of the water. The old Asian lady said, "Turn it over and see what prize you've won."

Jenny turned the fish over. "Number one," she said, "my lucky number."

The lady seemed as excited as Jenny. "Top-shelf winner! Choose your prize."

The top shelf was full of large stuffed animals. In the corner was a small colorful stuffed turtle. Jenny pointed at it and said, "That's my turtle."

The granny stepped up on a small stool to reach the turtle and handed it to Jenny. "Good luck for you. Painted turtle means new love."

William loved Jenny's boundless enthusiasm, especially when she snuggled up to him and gave him a big kiss on the cheek. At that point, he knew that catching that little wooden fish meant more to him than the bonefish he had lost that morning.

CHAPTER 11

THE CASTING LESSON

Still holding hands, they walked to Jenny's Jeep and climbed in: William, Jenny, and her turtle.

"Where to, madam?" he asked, trying to sound like Shay, his chauffeur.

"You've got to get up early tomorrow, Will," she said, "so I think it's best that you take me home."

"Where's home?"

"Mrs. Reno's house," she said. "It's right next to her Conch Bar."

"Mrs. Reno's?" he asked.

"My dad's been bringing me down here to fish since I was a little girl. We always stayed at the Lookout Lodge Resort, and that's how I got to know Mrs. Reno. She's always treated me like a daughter and started inviting me to stay with her when I came to the Keys by myself."

Halfway home, Jenny said, "You're an angler?"

"I can't even get a fly out of the boat. I don't know what I was thinking."

"So if you're not an angler, Will, what are you?"

"Well, yesterday I was the Man of the Year," he said.

"And what are you today?" she asked.

"The waiter," he said.

"At least you're multifaceted," she said.

Jenny directed him to Mrs. Reno's driveway. They pulled up to the house and William turned off the lights, took the key out of the ignition, and handed it to her.

"Thanks for the great evening," he said, turning to walk back to his dad's house.

"Not yet," Jenny whispered. "Follow me. I want to show you something." They walked around the house and out to a small moonlit beach with a beach hammock hung between two palm trees. The music from next door had stopped. The only noise they could hear was the water lapping gently on the shore.

"Look out there," Jenny said, pointing to the water. "What do you see?"

William searched the horizon and saw a channel marker blinking red way off in the distance, probably on the inland waterway.

"That blinking marker?" he asked.

"No," she said. "Look carefully at the water. See it?"

And he did. The water was glowing incandescent green.

"What is it?"

"It's luminescence," she said. "It happens some nights when the conditions are right. I knew it would happen tonight."

Jenny stepped in front of him, put her hands on his chest, and said, "Now, what's wrong with your cast?"

"My cast? I don't know. My father and that asshole fishing guide of his—"

"Shh," she quieted him. "Don't worry about them. Turn around. Turn your back to me."

He smiled and did what she said. Gently she put her left hand on the small of his back and her right hand on the back of his right arm. She touched him so gently William had to take a breath.

"Now show me your cast," she said.

"But I don't have a fly rod," he said.

"You don't need one, Will. Show me."

He started making a casting motion. She gently guided his elbow higher.

"Good," she said, "but your body is tense. Relax. Breathe. Forget I'm even here."

"Yeah, right," he said.

"Do you have a favorite song?" she asked.

"Yeah, 'Unforgettable.' Your version."

She let that slide. "Close your eyes and sing it. Listen to the music in your head."

He closed his eyes and continued making a casting motion with his body. William began to sing the lyrics to "Unforgettable." As he did, he felt his body begin to relax. He became more fluid and more comfortable.

"Good," Jenny whispered, then touched the back of his neck as he continued to sing quietly and cast. Her fingers moved down to his lower back and then around his waist. He cast again and she slowly pressed her body against his.

He couldn't take it anymore. He turned around and leaned down to kiss her. She touched her finger to his mouth and said, smiling, "You need to practice."

"But—"

"But maybe I'll see you tomorrow night after dinner, at Mrs. Reno's, and maybe you'll ask me to dance."

She turned to walk back to Mrs. Reno's house, stopping for a moment to say, "Thanks for the turtle."

His head was spinning. He hardly remembered walking back to his dad's house. The porch light was on and the couch was made into a bed. He turned the light off without taking off his clothes and, with a now familiar favorite song in his head, fell fast asleep.

CHAPTER 12

DAY TWO— THE TARPON

"Up'n at 'em, son," Leo said as he tried to shake William to life. The smell of bacon frying aided his father's mission. Lying on the couch on his stomach, William turned his head toward his father's voice and peeked out with one eye. The early-morning sun streaming through the living room window hit him, causing him to groan.

"Don't you fishermen ever sleep in a little?" he asked his father.

"Not and catch fish we don't," Leo said. "C'mon, shake it off, go on into the john and freshen up. I let you sleep as long as I could, we've got forty-five minutes to eat some breakfast and get to the dock. Still like your eggs scrambled, a little runny?"

"How did you remember that?"

"I remember a lot of things," his father said as he walked out the door.

To save time, William stripped down to his underwear, splashed some water on his face, checked to see that his bandage was still in place, brushed his teeth, and sprayed on some deodorant. He had a bad case of bed-head but decided he'd let it go till later.

He walked out to the living room barefoot and put on the other shorts he'd bought along with the T-shirt that said ISLAMORADA—A SMALL DRINKING TOWN WITH A BIG FISHING PROBLEM.

His father laughed when he read his shirt.

"Do you have an extra baseball cap I can borrow?"

"Sure," Leo said, "you'll find a few hanging on the living room door. I'm going to leave old Dorado locked up in the backyard today. He's such a beggar around the marina, and those damn tourists can't resist him. French fries are his favorite. Even has his own bowl of water by the bar. Sometimes the boys will fill it up with beer. The old hound just loves cold Budweiser, almost as much as I used to."

His father had prepared a big platter of scrambled eggs to go along with bacon and a bowl of grits. He also brought out a small basket of biscuits and a jar of strawberry jam. William cleaned his plate twice as though he'd never seen food before.

They left the dishes in the sink before turning Dorado loose in the backyard. William grabbed a wide-brimmed fishing hat. His father brought out his favorite tarpon rod and they put out a large bowl of water in the backyard for the dog before they headed for the marina.

On the way, William's father told him a little about tarpon. "We call them silver kings. They're our biggest and fiercest target species in the backcountry. They range up to two hundred pounds . . . ugly prehistoric fish with a protruding jaw and huge eyes. They're tough as hell to hook because their mouths are as smooth and hard as the porcelain bowl of a toilet.

"When you're lucky enough to hook one, they go ballistic and spend more time outta the water than in it. They're tireless fighters. People come from all around the world to take one on. Just seeing one jump is enough for a lot of anglers."

They pulled up at 7:45 a.m. Cole was busying himself loading up ice, water, and the lunches. He managed a muffled "hello" when they said good morning. *Progress*, William thought, as Cole assured Leo that he'd already picked up a score sheet and tourney-supplied camera.

They motored out to the harbor for their 8:00 a.m. departure. As they sat among the other boats waiting for the send-off, Bobby yelled over, "Hey, waiter, can I borrow your mobile phone? I need to make an important call."

Everyone within earshot laughed, including William.

Mrs. Reno walked on the dock with Jenny beside her, looking lovely in white shorts and a blue spaghetti-strapped blouse.

Mrs. Reno cleared her throat and spoke into the microphone. "Welcome to day two of the tournament.

To give you the leader update, we're privileged to have with us one of the tournament founders, a doctor, International Game Fish Association record holder, and a woman *Saltwater Magazine* described as one of the finest anglers in the world, Jenny Hunter!"

The crowd cheered and whistled and someone let out a huge catcall.

"Behave, boys," Mrs. Reno said, handing the mike to Jenny.

Jenny smiled and waved to the rowdy anglers. "Thank you all for participating in this tournament." A few more whistles ensued before Jenny started up again. "Yesterday was a good first day, but no team caught more than one of the targeted species, though I did hear through the grapevine that yesterday numerous barracuda, bonnethead sharks, and even a Northeastern mobile phone were released."

The skiffs erupted with laughter. *God*, William thought, *is there anyone in Islamorada who hasn't heard about my mobile phone?*

"At present," Jenny continued, "thirty-nine teams are tied for the lead with one qualifying fish. It's anyone's game. So good luck to you all and don't forget the party tonight at Mrs. Reno's and catch 'em up. Tight lines!"

Mrs. Reno gave a blast on her air horn and yelled, "Go fishin'!"

Idling out in the channel, William said to his dad, "She's pretty special, isn't she?"

"Jenny?" he asked. "Yeah, I've known her for a long time. She used to come down here with her dad, a retired doc. He pulled a hook out of my thumb one day at the dock. Didn't hurt a bit. Cole used to take her and her dad fishing."

"Far and away the best woman angler who's fished on my boat," Cole said. Then off they went, only this time William remembered to stay seated and to turn his borrowed hat around.

Today they ran south for an hour to a place called Nine Mile Bank. Leo told William it was a great place to ambush tarpon. They might see some bonefish or permit there, too.

Arriving at Nine Mile, Cole turned off the engine and climbed up on the poling platform with his push pole in hand. He pushed the boat forward over the flat. Reaching the edge, where a six-foot-deep channel ran by the bank, he stuck one end of the pole into the sand and tied the other to a line attached to his platform.

"Don't we pole around and look for them?" William asked him.

"No, we stake up here and wait for them to come to us," Cole said, scanning the horizon as two other skiffs pulled in, being careful to keep their distance so as not to interfere with each other. The boat next to them belonged to Bobby.

Leo stood up, stretched, and pulled his tarpon rod out from under the gunnel. William stood, too, and assumed his usual position sitting on the cooler.

"Not today," Leo said. "Get up here and take this rod. You're the angler today."

William stepped up to the bow and started pulling off some line as he'd learned the day before. This rod was much heavier than the one they'd used yesterday. Slowly and awkwardly, he started practicing his casting with Cole looking on from the poling platform and his father standing just behind him.

"Don't rush your release," Leo said.

William tried it and the line got caught up on itself, dropping into the water next to the boat.

Bobby yelled over, "Hey, Cole, forget about changing flies, you better change your angler!"

"Hey, Bobby," Cole said. "I think I might have left a pair of handcuffs at your house. Ask your wife if she knows where they are."

Bobby flipped Cole the bird and Cole growled, "Leo, take the goddamn rod back and let the cooler bitch sit his ass back down on the ice chest."

"You know the rules, Cole," he said, "he has to catch at least one of the qualifying fish."

"You both know I can hear you, right?" William said.

"Just relax, kid," his dad said. "Take a breath and start over again."

As William practiced, Cole continued to scan the water. They were there for an hour before they saw anything. Three southbound tarpon swam by them, but over along the far edge of the channel, too far away and moving too fast to cast at.

So it went for another hour as the hot sun beat down on Team McKay. Finally, Cole said, "Let's move, it's not happening here today. I want to check out Schooner."

"Where's that?" William asked.

"It's another bank about six miles from here," Leo said. As Cole prepared to leave, William noticed that several of the other boats staked up near theirs were coming to the same conclusion and preparing to leave.

The wind was beginning to pick up out of the northeast. Leo told William that was good for fishing. "In most fisheries, west is best," he said, "because it's the prevailing wind direction. Here, our prevailing winds are out of the northeast and that's when our fish are most comfortable and eat best."

Schooner Bank was quiet as well. If these fish were getting comfortable with anything, it seemed to be avoiding them. William used the time to practice his casting on the bow.

Cole said, "Let's slide over to Ox Foot. It's a little closer to the ocean and gets some good fish this time of the year. Just gotta watch those big sharks over there."

As they made their move, two boats jumped in behind them in their wake. One of them was Bobby. They reached their destination and poled onto the shallow edge of the channel. Once again, Bobby poled in right next to them.

"Boy, Cole," William said, "that guy loves spending time with you."

"Yeah," Cole said. "He knows I know where the fish are, and if they're not around, he just likes to give me a raft of shit. He's a real pain in the ass."

As Cole climbed the tower, Leo sat on the cooler and insisted that William get back on the bow. "I've got a good feeling," he said.

William went back to practice casting while Cole scanned the water. Thirty minutes into his vigil, he shouted out, "Two tarpon coming at eleven o'clock!"

William struggled to retrieve his line, some of which had become tangled in his feet.

"Come on, kid, straighten out that mess," Leo said. "Where are they, Cole?"

"One's already gone, but the other is laid up at ten o'clock about fifty feet out. Leo, hurry that guy up for Christ's sake. This fish is going to bolt."

Finally, William got his line untangled. Leo said, "Cast now"—he pointed toward nine o'clock—"right there."

William closed his eyes, took a deep breath, and exhaled. As he started his casting motion, he began to sing "Unforgettable" under his breath.

"What the hell's he doing?" Cole asked.

"I think he's singing," Leo said.

Ignoring them both, William had his line forming a perfect loop in the air. Staying with the rhythm of his song, he cast his line to exactly where his father had pointed and watched the large yellow fly drop safely in the water.

"Oh my God!" Cole said.

His fly sank right in front of a six-foot tarpon suspended about three feet below the surface. Its large silver scales gleamed like radiant armor in the refracted sunlight. William thought he saw its eyes scanning for movement in the water.

"Start stripping line in, but not too fast," Leo said.

Still singing, William began to strip line. He could see the big tarpon look right at his fly. Then, suddenly, like a silver torpedo, the tarpon's body surged forward. Opening its large, gaping lower jaw like a bucket, it inhaled the fly.

William's rod jerked in his hands as the tarpon exploded vertically out of the water and thrashed the air twenty feet away from the skiff.

"Holy shit!" William said.

"Lower your rod tip!" Cole shouted. "Lower your rod tip!"

William did so as the big fish crashed back into the water.

"Whenever he jumps, lower the tip," his father said.

"I thought I was supposed to keep it tight?"

"You are," Leo said, "but not when he jumps. He's too big; he'll break you off in the air. You point the rod tip down to give him some slack till he's back in the water. It's called bowing to the king."

The tarpon surged and jumped again. William lowered the rod tip and his father said, "Good."

The tarpon started to run, taking back line as it went. William noticed that everyone in the nearby skiffs was paying attention.

As line flew off the reel, he asked, "What do I do now?"

"Nothing," his father said, "just keep the rod tip up to keep some pressure on him. He's still green and you can't stop him. We'll go after him."

Cole pulled up the push pole, jumped off the tower, and stowed the pole on the gunnel. Then he started the engine, put it in gear, and began following the tarpon as the knobs on William's reel spun and line continued to fly off.

"Get ready to reel as fast as you can," Cole said. "We're going to give you some slack as we catch up with him."

All of a sudden William's reel stopped turning. "He's not running anymore," he said.

Cole and Leo looked at each other and in unison said, "Reel, reel, reel."

"Feel anything yet, any pressure?" Leo asked.

"Nothing yet," he said, still reeling frantically.

Cole turned off the engine and climbed back on the tower to see what was going on.

"He's charging right at us," Cole yelled. "Keep reeling! Catch up to him! Faster! He's almost here. Leo, grab the camera. I may get a chance to touch the leader, qualifying it as a catch."

Then it got frantic. With Cole and Leo scurrying around the boat, William reeled in line as quickly as he could. When the line grew tight, he lifted the rod.

Looking into the water, he said, "Oh shit," as he saw the big fish streaming right at them. At the last moment, the tarpon exploded out of the water and smashed into the bow of the boat. The impact caused William to lose his balance, and he fell overboard. Bobbing to the surface, he could see Cole grabbing the leader and his father taking a picture of the dazed fish as it lay momentarily by the side of the boat.

"That's an official catch and release!" Cole shouted.

The dazed fish came to and surged away from the boat again. Feeling pressure on the rod in his hands, William yelled, "He's still on, he's still on!"

Several of the anglers and guides in the nearby skiffs, including Bobby, let out a great cheer.

"Atta boy," Leo said, "you're doing good. Keep on lifting up and reeling down."

"We got the catch," Cole said, "break him off."

"No way," William said, "I want to land this fish."

Suddenly, the dark dorsal fin of a bull shark sliced the surface of the water off the bow and swam right past William in hot pursuit of the tarpon, which had revived and was now pulling out more line.

"Shit," Cole said. "That must have been what turned him around."

Leo leaned over the side of the boat toward William. "Give me your hand, let it go."

"Fuck the shark,"William said. "I'm gonna land this fish!"

"Give me your hand right now!"

William turned his back to the boat to face the fleeing fish and felt four strong hands grabbing him out of the water, tossing him onto the gunnel near the stern of the skiff.

"Get your feet inside this boat!" Leo said. William scrambled to his feet, still holding the rod. He felt the fish begin to rise and watched as his tarpon jumped high in the air, its silver scales flashing. But this time it didn't matter that William bowed to the fish. As its magnificent, elegant body hit the water, it was torn in half by the jaws of the bull shark.

"No!"William shouted. Blood erupted and clouded the brilliant water as the huge bull shark seized and shook the tarpon's thrashing remains.

William dropped the rod in the boat and pushed past Cole to grab his push pole. He saw the dark eyes of the shark as it finished off the tarpon. It seemed to look at William.

"You son of a bitch!" William shouted. "That was my fish!" He started stabbing at the shark with the sharp end of the pole. He kept on stabbing him until it was gone, leaving only a pool of red blood in the water.

He stood, panting and soaked to the bone. Cole and Leo and the men on the other boats were silent, all eyes on William.

"What's the matter?" William asked, breaking the silence.

"Nothing," Cole said. "Nothing at all. Good catch, I guess. We got our tarpon."

"Yeah," Leo said extending his hand. "Good job, son."

"Had enough for the day, Leo?" Cole asked. "Wanna head in?"

"Good idea," Leo said. "Let's head for the dock."

William was shivering with cold on the way in as they flew over the sea of grass that was called the back-country. But his adrenaline was still pumping, and it felt good. It wasn't till then that he realized that he'd lost another hat.

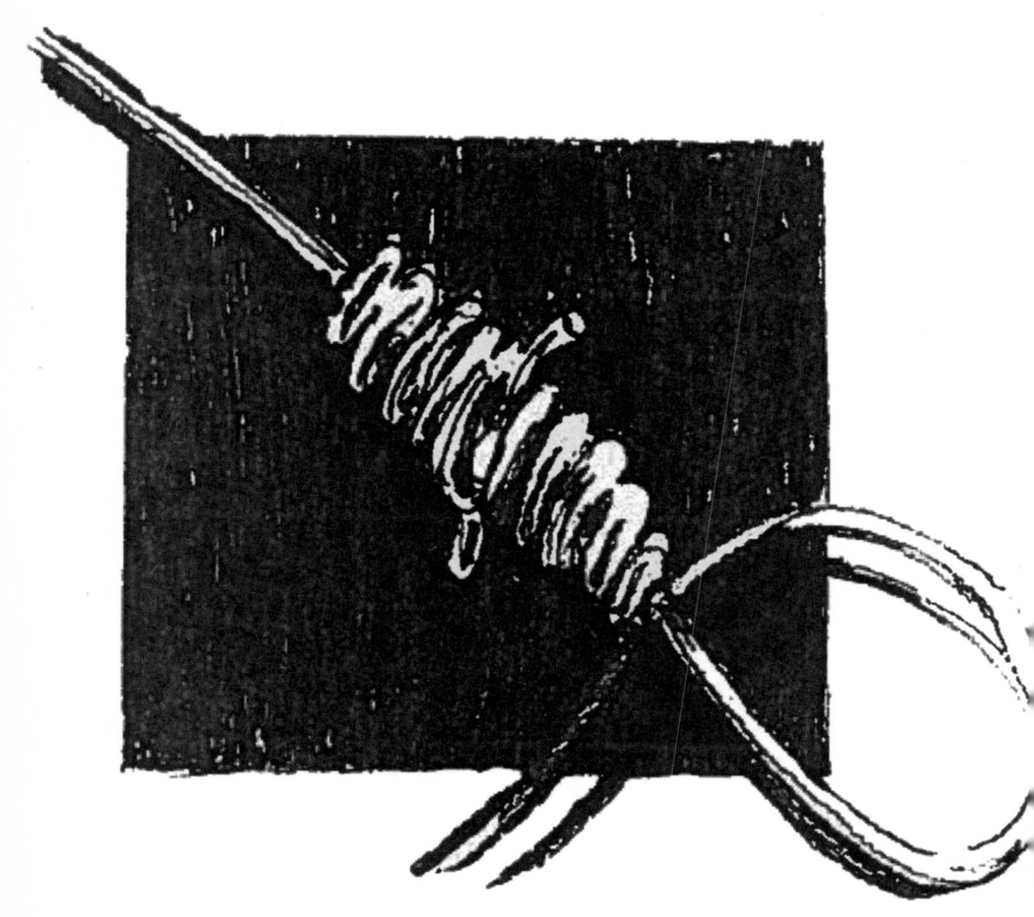

CHAPTER 13

THE BLOOD KNOT

William and Leo drove home together, not saying much. William knew that his father was happy but didn't think he looked well. His coloring was poor and he was coughing a lot and rubbing hard on the inside of his arm.

"You all right, Dad?"

"Just a little tired, I think."

"Me, too," he said, "and I can't wait to get out of these damp shorts. The boys got wet and they're itching like crazy."

Leo laughed. "Son, you've got a condition that all men hate. You've got a case of DWB."

William cocked an eyebrow at his father.

"Dreaded Wet Balls."

They were still laughing as they pulled into the driveway. Leo was looking better.

William made a beeline for the shower and came out of the bathroom feeling much better. He found his dad sitting on the porch, smoking a cigarette and tying up some fishing line.

"You know, Dad," William said, "maybe in deference to your health, you ought to quit smoking."

"Kid, that's why I quit the booze. Can only stop one thing at a time. Maybe I can get to cigarettes next."

"What are you doing with that fishing line?"

"I'm tying up some permit leaders," he said. "I could buy 'em at the Outfitters but I like to tie them myself so I know they're done right and less likely to break."

"What's that knot?"

"That's a blood knot. It's used to connect different strength lines or lines that have been broken. If it's tied correctly, the connection can make the line stronger than before it was severed."

William watched his father's sun-spotted old hands weave the two pieces of line deftly as if he'd done it many, many times before. Then Leo cinched the two lines together, forming a beautiful barrel-like knot.

"Here, you try it," he said, handing William two pieces of line.

Leo watched as his son struggled.

"No, go under there with the tag line," he said, "then cinch it down tight." Looking at William's finished product, Leo smiled and said, "Not bad, not bad. You see, broken things can be mended."

William knew that his father wasn't just talking about the line, but he didn't want to go there right now. He sat back and looked out over his father's tiny front lawn overlooking the quiet street.

"You know," the old man said, "a bull shark is nothin' to mess around with."

"Neither am I," William said.

His dad smiled.

"That was something, fighting that big tarpon," William said. "I knew that fish wasn't going to beat me."

Leo looked off into the distance, then said, "A long time ago, I hooked a blue marlin about sixty miles away from here off the Cay Sal Bank. It was the biggest fish I've ever seen. Must have gone thirteen hundred . . . fourteen hundred pounds. I thought my heart would stop just looking at her. I fought that fish in the rain for four and a half hours.

"She jumped like ten times and when she came down, the waves would drop out beneath her and leave a huge hole in the sea. It was as if, when she was in the air, the ocean missed her presence. Then she'd crash down again and the spray would go flying."

With trembling hands, Leo lit another cigarette.

"That year, I was at my lowest. My money was worthless. My power was worthless. I couldn't breathe. Nothing would alter the decisions I'd made that got me there. But everything changed when I fought that magnificent beast. She didn't care who I was or how much money I had. She didn't care about my accomplishments or my failures. She didn't care if I was a good man or a bad man."

He took a long pull on his cigarette.

"As you might have felt today, a fish fight is in the moment. You're engaged in a pure test of strength and will and luck and skill and—"

"Honor?"

"Yes, honor," Leo said, "or the lack of it. Being who I was then, I would have killed that marlin if I'd caught her, but that would have been the end of me. Luckily, after all that time, she beat me. I slacked the line for an instant and lost the fish. It was the best thing that could have ever happened to me. Sometimes we lose, son, and it makes us better men."

"What's that knot called again?" William asked him.

"A blood knot," he said.

"You going to Mrs. Reno's party tonight?" William asked.

"No, I don't think so," he said. "I'm hoping to get some solid sleep tonight. I've been tired lately."

"How about some food?" William asked.

"Sure," he said, "I could eat. How about I show you the Islamorada Fishing Club?"

CHAPTER 14

THE TRUTH

As they started the short ride to the club, Leo told William about the third fish on their target list.

"The toughest fish to catch with a fly rod is the permit. They're also one of the scarcest, so a lot of people don't even try. They're members of the pompano family, silver like a bonefish and oblong shaped. You often find them schooled up on wrecks in the ocean, but out there in the deeper water they'll reject every fly in your kit.

"They come into the backcountry to feed on the flats. They love sun, sand bottoms, and crabs. They also have an uncanny ability to stay just outside your casting range. Perhaps their most distinctive characteristic is their huge eyes, which give them incredible eyesight. When you finally do get a shot at one, he'll tail down and stare at your fly for the longest time. If they see something they don't like, *poof*, they're gone. If you do get one on, he'll pull like a small freight train—never jump, just pull. We'll be lucky to see one, let alone catch one tomorrow. The big weather front that's coming through in the morning won't help."

As the sun set over the backcountry, they pulled into a small parking lot of the Islamorada Fishing Club. Inside, the club had restaurant seating for about sixty and some outdoor seating overlooking a harbor full of boats of all sizes. The most prominent feature was a horse-shoe-shaped bar, where the bartender and the patrons all seemed to know one another. The dark wood walls were covered with big fish mounts and pictures of members proudly showing off their prize catches on docks. Most of the photos dated back to a time when anglers killed everything they caught. Tonight, almost all the tables were full of sunburned anglers drinking, laughing, and eating.

The bar was two-deep with men William recognized as guides, and right in the middle of them was the ever-present Bobby. Everyone seemed to recognize William's father, welcoming him with a loud chorus of "Leo! Leo!" A few even clapped and cheered as father and son made their way to a small table in the corner. Leo responded with a bashful wave.

As they sat down, Leo said, "That applause was for you, William."

"Excuse me?"

"You made your mark out there today with that tarpon. I was proud of you."

"Thanks," William responded awkwardly, not knowing what else to say.

Just then, a freckled, fifty-something waitress with frizzy hair dropped off two glasses of ice water and greeted William's dad with, "Hiya, Leo. You gonna introduce me to this handsome son of yours?"

"Patti, this is my son, William."

"How ya doin', cutie?" she said, reaching out and shaking his hand, maybe for a bit too long.

"Can I get you boys something to drink?" she asked.

"A beer," William said, "something Mexican if you have it."

"How 'bout you, Leo, you drinkin' tonight?"

“I’ll stick with the water, thanks.”

“Sure, hon. I’ll be right back with that beer.”

William felt that this was his opportunity and he had to take it.

“Dad, why’d you walk out on us?”

The old man didn’t flinch. He took a deep breath as if he’d known the question was coming.

“I grew up feeling like I was in the shadow of your grandfather, who was a brilliant investment banker. No matter what I did, I couldn’t compete, couldn’t satisfy him. He second-guessed my every decision, always making me feel inadequate.

“The harder I tried, the worse it got, till I found myself thinking the only way things would change was by my leaving or his dying.”

Chirpy Patti brought William’s beer over, put it in front of him, and said, “Here’s looking up your record, sugar,” and walked away.

“And he died,” William said, remembering that overwhelming grief he’d felt as a teenager, losing his best friend.

“Yes. And it was good for a few years.”

“So why did you leave?”

“You came in and hit the street running, William,” he said. “It was your time. I knew you would do what was right for the business, make the decisions that I knew had to be made, but didn’t have the stamina to do myself anymore. I was tired. I didn't want to do to you what my father had done to me."

"So you abandoned us instead?"

"I got out of your way."

"That may have been noble of you, Dad. But what about Mom? When did you fall out of love with her?"

"William, I never fell out of love with your mother. She was my rock, the light of my life. She believed in me and gave me strength. She was always there for me."

"And you repaid by leaving?"

"When she developed Alzheimer's, I was devastated. At first it was small stuff—couldn't find her glasses, forgotten appointments. We made adjustments. Then all of a sudden, she went so fast. Finally she stopped recognizing me. I felt totally lost and alone. I'd lost my compass."

"So you left her when she needed you the most?"

"Kid, no good will come of this conversation. The past is past. It's best if it stays that way."

"You called me, remember?" William shot back.

"Yeah, well," Leo stammered, "I just . . . this tournament came up and I thought, what the hell. So I called you."

"That's it?" he said. "No particular reason. Just 'what the hell'? . . . end of story?"

"No. We're having dinner together. That's something."

"Hey, look at this!" shouted Bobby, swaggering over toward their table like a drunken sea lion. Looking at

William, he said, "Buddy, that was quite a little show you put on out there today."

"I'm glad you were entertained," William said.

"Hell yes," Bobby slobbered, "but I think you mighta made your little brother jealous."

"Bobby!" Leo barked.

"What's he talking about, Dad?"

"Bobby, you shut your drunkard mouth!" his father yelled.

"What?" Bobby said, a look of drunken realization blooming across his face. "Are you tellin' me he doesn't know, Leo?"

Leo jumped up and grabbed Bobby by the throat. "Bobby Pinder, you get outta here before I do something awful."

Leo let go and Bobby stepped back, adjusted his collar, and staggered toward the men's room.

Leo sat back down.

"What the hell was that all about, Dad?"

"Nothing," he said.

"That was *not* nothing," William said.

"I don't want to talk about it."

William felt his blood begin to boil and slammed his fist down on the tabletop so hard that his father's water glass fell off the table and smashed on the floor.

By now, several of the other patrons were looking at them. "You're going to tell me what he was talking about and you're going to tell me right now."

With shaky hands, Leo started to light a cigarette. William grabbed it out of his hand and threw it aside.

"Now," William demanded, "or I'm on the next plane out of here and you can leave me in the past for good."

Leo sighed. "I have another son, William."

William felt rage rising through his body.

"Cole," Leo said.

William jumped up, knocking his chair over. "You were screwing his mother while you were married to Mom?"

Leo looked down at his hands as William headed for the door.

CHAPTER 15

THE CONFRONTATION

Still in a rage, William stormed out the front door of the club and started walking toward the highway. He'd gotten about a block away when one of the young guides he'd met pulled up to him in his truck, rolled down the window, and said, "Hi, William, where ya goin', need a lift?"

"I sure do," William said, "how about Mrs. Reno's place?"

The young man said, "Sure, hop in."

When they got to Mrs. Reno's, William stomped down the now familiar wooden plank pathway that wound through the mangroves to the bar. He could hear the sound of live music somewhere in the distance.

The big tournament party was in full swing, the thatch-roofed beach bar filled to capacity with partying anglers and guides. Still full of rage, William scanned the crowd for Jenny. Eventually he saw her dancing with some guy; their eyes met and she smiled at William. Then when her dance partner turned her with the music, William could see who she was dancing with: Cole.

He felt his fists knot up and his knuckles turn white. He stormed across the beach and across the dance floor.

As William approached, Cole said, "Hey, if it isn't the swimming waiter . . ."

But before he'd quite finished, William punched Cole with all his might square on the bridge of his nose.

Jenny screamed as Cole hit the deck and the dance floor cleared. Blood spurted from Cole's nose.

"You got anything else funny to say?" William shouted at him.

Cole got to his feet and charged, putting his shoulder into William's gut. William was knocked backward and Cole tagged him with an uppercut to the chin. Now it was his turn to hit the floor with the taste of blood in his mouth.

William jumped up and grabbed Cole and they went at it, punching, kicking, and eventually falling to the floor in a heap. Next thing he knew, William looked up and saw Mrs. Reno standing over them with a fire extinguisher. She pulled the plug and blasted them both.

Cole and William disengaged, coughing and gasping to get their breath. Mrs. Reno threw down the fire extinguisher and grabbed both of them by their shirt collars.

"What the hell's wrong with you two?" Mrs. Reno asked.

"He started it," Cole said.

"He what?" she shot back. "What are you—two ten-year-olds? Now shake hands."

William thought, *Now, that's not going to happen*, and knew from Cole's glare that was what he was thinking, too.

"I said, shake hands," Mrs. Reno said.

"No way," Cole and William said almost in unison.

"Well then get out," she said. "This is my bar and children don't belong at a bar. One of you go one way and one the other."

William took a few steps backward and turned and headed for the path. In the parking lot he saw Jenny arranging her luggage in the back of her rental Jeep. He was filthy and embarrassed and the cut on his forehead had opened up again. He felt blood running down the side of his face, but had no time to get cleaned up—he had to talk to her now.

She turned and seemed startled to see him, wiping a tear from her eye.

"Are you all right?" he asked her.

"No, William, I am not," she said.

"Please listen to me, Jenny," he said. "What happened back there had nothing to do with you."

"I don't care what it was," she said. "It was ugly and violent and it scared me. I thought that I made it pretty clear to you . . ."

"Where are you going?" he interrupted, not sure he wanted to hear the answer.

"I'm driving up to Fort Lauderdale to see if I can get on the earliest flight out to the Bahamas," she said. "I was supposed to leave this morning but I put my departure back a few days and now for the life of me, I can't remember why."

She climbed in the driver's-side door and started her engine.

"C'mon, Jenny," William said, grasping for straws, "what's this about?"

She looked him in the eye through the window and said, "Let's just say I've known more than enough violent men."

"Listen, Jenny," he said, "I may be a lot of things but I'm not that guy. How about I drive up to Lauderdale and keep you company?"

"No, Will," she said. "You may think you're not that guy, but you sure look like him to me . . . I need some time by myself to think. Someday if you ever discover who you are you can look me up."

Putting the vehicle in gear, she said, "And you've opened that cut on your forehead again and I thought I told you not to go swimming for a few days." With that, she backed the Jeep out of its space, spun the wheel, and drove away.

Watching her taillights pull away and fade into the darkness, William had never felt more alone in his life. Not knowing where to go, he skirted Mrs. Reno's bar and walked over to the little beach where Jenny had given him his casting lesson. The moon was high, the waves soft. Suddenly, he felt tired, tired of everything. He climbed into the hammock that swung gently in the breeze and in no time at all fell fast asleep.

CHAPTER 16

DAY THREE—THE PERMIT

William awoke in the morning with light drops of rain on his face. He decided to head to the marina, not knowing why or what he'd do when he got there; he didn't want to be a quitter and leave this way. He felt he needed closure even if it meant saying good-bye to his father and telling his newfound brother to piss off.

He hitched a ride over to the Lorelei with a fireman on his way to work. The guy looked at William and said, "None of my business, pal, you look like you had quite a night. I hope you got a few shots in on the other guy," and laughed.

"I'd call it a draw," William said, staring ahead as the windshield wipers tried to keep up with the now steady rain.

William arrived at the marina to see that most of the skiffs had left the dock but a few stragglers were loading up equipment, drinks, and lunches. Cole and

Leo, both in full rain gear, were sitting in the boat facing each other and working on some tackle in silence. Cole's nose was bruised and his face was swollen.

William heard Cole say to Leo, "What are we waiting for? You said he didn't even come home last night. Just tell the officials he's sick and let's go the hell fishing."

William's father said, "No."

"What do you mean, no?" Cole snapped. "I'm telling you he's gone. Probably hopped on his private jet and flew back to his big mountain of money."

"No," Leo said again.

"You should just cut bait with that spoiled brat and—"

Leo interrupted him and shouted, "No, goddamn it, Cole. He's my son as much as you are and I'm not leaving him, not again."

William couldn't take any more, so he walked over and as plainly as he could said, "You both know I can hear you, right?"

Their heads both swung around to look at him. The look of hatred on Cole's bruised face was counterbalanced by the look on his dad's that showed how happy he was to see him.

Leo said, "I knew you'd be here, son. I've brought extra rain gear for you in my duffel bag. Put it on and let's get going."

"Great!" Cole said. "What a fuckin' wasted day this'll be."

William climbed aboard and off they went in silence. They ran south for a while before Cole turned left and ran past a dockside restaurant on the left called Papa Joe's under the Indian Key Bridge, then past Bud and Mary's Marina. They drove through a channel and out into the ocean, where Cole turned right and headed down the shoreline for a place called Long Key. Once there, he cut the engine and poled onto a white sand flat. Remembering his conversation with his father the night before about permit, William guessed that Cole felt they'd have a decent chance to see one here.

Once there, Leo took his position on the bow with William right behind him and Cole standing vigil on the poling platform. William could feel Cole's eyes burning holes in his back. He didn't care; he was watching his father letting out line and taking a few practice casts. The rain was coming down heavily now, but even in the downpour and at seventy-five years of age, Leo's casting looked graceful and effortless.

Rain pelted the surface and turned the water murky with sand and silt. Ominous thunder rolled in the background, sometimes preceded by jagged bolts of lightning. Catching a permit under these conditions, William thought, might be mission impossible.

It didn't help that Cole was ignoring the job at hand and glaring at William from his perch.

"Hold on," Leo said. "I think I see a spiky little tail over by that mangrove shoot."

William wondered if it was wishful thinking by the old man, and Cole must have been feeling the same way because William was sure that no one on Cole's boat had ever spotted a fish before he did. But Leo cast anyway and laid a crab fly down softly in the vicinity of where he said he'd seen a tail.

Holding his rod tip down, he bumped the fly once and a large oblong-shaped fish pounced all over it. He came tight immediately and arched his rod as the big permit took off across the flat, fighting to reach deeper water.

"Stick it to 'em!" Cole said, jumping down from the platform. "This is our tournament-winning fish. Nobody could've caught anything sooner in this weather. Keep some good pressure and don't let him get over that edge."

Leo played the fish perfectly and had it up to the side of the boat in about fifteen minutes. Cole grabbed the net, and William grabbed the camera. Then Cole scooped the fish into the boat on the first try and laid it on the deck for William to photograph. He held the big permit up for Leo's inspection.

William and Cole thought the old man must be thrilled but when he turned his weather-beaten face toward them they could see, despite the rain, that he'd been crying.

"Gotta be thirty pounds, congratulations," William said, trying to lighten the moment. But immediately Leo seemed to be seized by a sharp and sudden pain. His eyes became glassy as his fishing rod fell out of his wrinkled hands and he clutched his chest.

"Dad!" Cole and William said in unison and rushed to the bow to catch him as he collapsed.

With rain falling in his pale eyes, he looked up at their bruised faces and said in a whisper, "My boys . . . my wild, wild boys." Their father's eyes fixed in the distance.

• • •

Back in the little rowboat, in the middle of Loch Loon with their fishing lines in the water, William turned his head so that his young grandson wouldn't see his tears.

"Did your dad die, Grandpa?" Kyle asked him.

"Yes, yes he did, Kyle," he told him. "Leo Burns McKay, my father, your great-grandfather."

"I'm so sorry, Grandpa," the boy said. "I know what it feels like to be abandoned by your father."

This snapped William from his sadness, and he said, "Kyle, my father never abandoned me, and neither did yours. Things happened in their lives that they couldn't handle, but it was not us they were running from."

"That's what Mom says, too," Kyle said, "but I keep thinking maybe if I'd done more around the house or worked harder in school or did better in sports . . . maybe my dad wouldn't have left me."

"Listen, Kyle, you're a good person on the way to becoming a fine young man. Part of growing up is learning that some things are out of our control and they just happen. The mark of a good man or a good woman is how they deal with adversity."

"What do you mean, Grandpa?"

"Well, things happen in people's lives that they just can't handle. Sometimes married people grow apart. This isn't about you. As hard as it seems, you just have to be there for your mom and for your dad."

"But it's not fair!" Kyle said.

"I know how you feel, son, but no one ever said that life is fair."

"But," the boy said with tears welling up in his eyes, "I love my dad and I thought he loved me. We used to go places together and do things together and talk. He used to call me his best buddy. Then he just left. We didn't talk about it at all. He just did it."

Kyle was crying hard, now. "He'll probably get married again and have more children . . . another best buddy, and he'll forget all about me. It just makes me so angry that I never want to talk to him again."

"Listen, Kyle, you will always be his firstborn and he'll always love you," William said. "If you don't mind a little advice from someone who knows, don't shut him out of your heart and don't judge him. Just try to understand him and talk to him about how you feel. It will help you. I know. My father hurt me, and I got angry with him and lost a lot of time that we could have been friends. I'll always regret that."

Kyle calmed a little, sniffled twice, ran the back of his hand across his eyes, and cleared his throat. The water lapped against the boat, and something about the peaceful sound stopped his crying altogether.

After a long while, Kyle sensed William needed to get back to his story, so he said, "What happened next in the Keys, Grandpa?"

William was suddenly very proud of how the boy was able to look beyond his own hurt. He was growing up just fine.

"Well, we did all we could think of to save our dad," William said. "Cole grabbed his VHF radio and called the coast guard, throwing the permit back in the water as they patched us through to a nine-one-one operator. We arranged to rush him to the closest dock to our location and the EMT was there as we pulled in. Their team leader checked his pulse, found none, and pronounced him dead on the scene. They transported his body to Mariners Hospital. Cole and I drove back to the dock in silence."

CHAPTER 17

THE REQUEST

The tournament was over. They'd won it and didn't even turn in their score sheets. The goal that the three of them had been pursuing for three days with such passion just didn't seem important anymore.

William drove his dad's truck over to his house and fed his dog. Like all great and loyal pets, Dorado seemed to know that something was wrong. Instead of going to his bed, the old dog went right over to Leo's favorite chair, flopped down in front of it, and waited, watching the front door.

William called his assistant, Arnelle, told her what happened, and asked her if she could help him with arrangements. Half an hour later, Arnelle called back and said that she had spoken with the local magistrate, a woman named Mrs. Reno, who knew all about what had happened. Mrs. Reno had also said that she was a friend of William's dad and that she had scheduled a memorial service three days from then at 3:00 p.m. at the Presbyterian church. She also wanted the two boys to meet her in her office afterward to go over the will.

"Okay," William told her, then asked if she would overnight him some clothes and have Captain Harding standing by at the Marathon Airport so he could get out of there ASAP after the meeting.

"Yes, sir," she said. "Anything else I can help you with?"

"Yeah," William said, "please call my friend Marty Cooper at Motorola, and tell him that they need to waterproof their mobile phones."

"What?" Arnelle said.

"Never mind," William said.

• • •

A funeral in a church was a real anomaly in the Keys, where most of the locals were cremated and their ashes scattered on the Florida Bay with a flotilla of boats carrying family, friends, and neighbors forming a waterbound congregation. Looking around the small Presbyterian church, it was obvious that many of the congregants had never been there before, except maybe for an occasional Christmas or Easter service.

Reverend Spalding presided over the service, and from his remarks, it was clear that Leo had been a stranger to him. Perhaps the world's worst choir was backed by an organist who must have been ninety-five years old. The highlight of the service was a harmonica solo of "Amazing Grace" by a guide friend of Leo's, Captain Jimmy Cauthorn.

Once the service was over, William headed to Mrs. Reno's. He had been dreading it all day but knew he had to be there. At the funeral he'd seen Cole across the aisle, but the two of them had ignored each other pretty much. William arrived first and was shown to a small upstairs office above the thatch-roofed gin mill. He could hear muffled music from the jukebox in the bar below. He looked around the office. On her desk was a small plaque that read: MRS. RENO—ISLAMORADA MAGISTRATE. Behind her desk on the wall was a beautiful mount of a jumping sailfish. Certificates of all kinds and pictures crowded her walls—pictures of Mrs. Reno with anglers, with fish, with dignitaries, and several with his dad and Cole.

Cole walked in with Mrs. Reno. She took her seat behind her desk while Cole and William sat in front of her like unruly kids called into the principal's office. Nothing was said.

Mrs. Reno stared at both of them for a moment. Eventually, she reached into a Publix Market shopping bag sitting beside her desk and pulled out a sealed bottle of Glenturret filled with ashes, with baling wire wound around the neck, fashioned into a handle.

She put the bottle on the desk right in front of the brothers and said, "There he is, just like he wanted, his ashes in a bottle of his favorite whiskey."

Neither man said anything.

"Are you two listening?" Mrs. Reno said.

"Yes," William said. Cole nodded almost imperceptibly.

"Excuse me, Cole, are you listening?" Mrs. Reno asked again.

"Yeah," Cole said. "Can we just get on with it?"

"It's your father's last wishes, for Christ's sake. You have somewhere important you need to be?"

This seemed to wake them both up a bit, and after a pause, Mrs. Reno began to read the letter.

"It is my last earthly wish that my cremated ashes will be scattered far offshore at Cay Sal Bank by my two sons."

"That's bullshit," Cole interrupted. "The old man must have been out of his mind! There's no way I'm takin' this cream puff to Cay Sal."

"The whole thing's ridiculous," William chimed in. "I'm leaving."

He stood up and reached across for the bottle of ashes on Mrs. Reno's desk.

Cole also jumped up and grabbed his wrist. "What the hell you think you're doing?" Cole shouted at him. "You ain't takin' that!"

"You better let go of my wrist, pal, while you still can," William said.

By now they were nose-to-nose, their father's ashes between them. "Nobody cares who you are here, rich boy," Cole growled. "You can't buy whatever you want, and you want to know the truth?"

"I think I've figured out the truth, you conch bastard," William shouted back.

"Well, the truth is, you're nothing," Cole said. "The only thing you got in this world is dough, and money don't mean shit to me. And it didn't mean shit to him, either, so you better believe me when I tell you, you're not taking his ashes."

"Shut up, Cole!" Mrs. Reno shouted. "Just shut up both of you. You both make me sick. Sick and sad. So the man had secrets; we've all got secrets. Does that mean you don't honor his last wishes? Nobody's perfect, nobody let alone the two of you it seems. But you could show some respect and maybe even a little compassion."

The two men stopped glaring at each other, and Cole finally let go of William's wrist.

"He was your father, for God's sake. You two need to bury the hatchet, if only for a day. Do right by your dad. If you can't do that, there's no hope for either of you."

Mrs. Reno picked up the bottle of ashes and put it in her desk drawer.

"Now you two go think about that. Think about what kind of men you are. His ashes will be here in the morning."

Evening was coming by the time William got back to his dad's place, and the crickets were already beginning to chirp. He stood looking at the old conch house for a while then loosened his tie and sat down on the front porch steps to think. Suddenly, the screen door creaked behind him, and he saw Dorado limping out onto the porch.

The old dog whimpered and William said, "Come here, boy." Dorado lowered his head and came over to him, flopped down and put his head in his lap. William held him close.

They stayed that way for a while until William pushed Dorado back toward the house and his bed in Leo's room. As they entered the bedroom, William flipped on the lights and was amazed at what he saw. Just as the walls of his father's bathroom were covered with pictures, so, too, were the walls of his bedroom. But these weren't fishing pictures—these were family pictures of them when they lived together. There were pictures of his mom and dad at their wedding, a picture of his father in his office on Wall Street, several formal pictures of them together—father, mother, and son. There was a picture of William at graduation from West Point, being confirmed at the church, and one of his dad and him fishing together in a small boat on a lake—Loch Loon.

William sat on his dad's bed with his head on his hands. Dorado stayed by his feet, looking up at the man crying.

• • •

Meanwhile, with the sun setting through broken clouds on the Florida Bay and gentle breezes blowing out of the southwest, Cole was alone on his skiff pulling crab traps.

He stood on the bow, reached over, and grabbed hold of a white marker buoy marked D&C. Hand over hand, he started retrieving the heavy line from the depths until he could pull in the wooden trap.

With the trap on his deck, he opened the lid and counted six large crabs inside. All of a sudden he stopped, almost as if someone had knocked the wind out of him.

He slumped to the floor of his skiff and slowly pulled a clipboard from his center console. On the clipboard was a tally sheet with two columns of handwritten numbers. The heading above one column read COLE and above the other, DAD.

Cole hugged the clipboard to his chest and buried his face in his arms.

• • •

The next morning William was up at dawn, dressed in fishing clothes. After putting Dorado out with food and water, he got in his dad's truck, made one stop at Mrs. Reno's, and then drove to the Lorelei. Deep blue stratus clouds drifted across a brilliant red sunrise as he walked straight to Cole's slip, carrying the bottle of his father's ashes and the rosewood dueling pistol box.

Cole had gotten up early, too. He was standing amid ten crab traps, which he had been scrubbing before putting them in storage.

Cole looked up at William carrying the bottle and asked, "How the hell'd you get that?"

"I promised Mrs. Reno I'd follow our father's last wish, today . . . now . . . and then I'm out of here."

"There's a storm coming and Cay Sal Bank is more than fifty miles away," Cole said, adding, "How's a tenderfoot like you gonna find his way out there and back?"

"Well, that's where you come in," William said. "You want to help me?"

Cole thought for a minute then said, "Sure. I've been thinking, too, and I can't let you do this without me."

"Well, let's go then," William said, "right now. Let's do this."

"Okay," Cole said, "but my boat's way too small for this trip. Dad had a thirty-four-footer that's parked on the other side of the harbor. I fueled it last week thinking he and I would go offshore fishing after that father–son tourney. It's an old clunker but should be able to make the trip."

Then he asked, "What's in the box?"

"It's . . . it's a surprise maybe for later," William answered.

"Well, let's go then," Cole said.

CHAPTER 18

CAY SAL BANK

On the other side of the harbor the old wooden boat with *Keys Disease* written across the transom sat bobbing in the water. *Appropriate name*, William thought. The two men climbed aboard, and William realized quickly that it was a spartan craft, with a fishing cockpit in the stern and one step up into a small salon with a couch. There were a few chairs and a tiny galley, and up front there was a single "stateroom" with two berths adjoining a small head.

The controls were up top on the bridge, which was accessed by climbing a six-stepped ladder. The boat also had outriggers on each side, long aluminum poles that were locked in the upward position but could be lowered to hold line for offshore fishing. It was the kind of boat northerners called a cabin cruiser but the locals called a sportfish.

Cole took the ashes, climbed up to the bridge, and fired up the single gas engine. It started right away but smoked badly. William cast off the lines and they were on their way.

Storm clouds were building on the horizon as they headed out to sea, Cole at the controls on the bridge and William standing in the cockpit. Laughing gulls flew over their outriggers, squawking as they passed the headpin. William looked back and saw Islamorada begin to disappear in the distance. He looked inside the salon and saw the rosewood box secure on one of the old chairs where he'd put it.

"I'm gonna have a drink," Cole shouted down, "how 'bout you?"

"Yeah, sure," William said, "why not?"

"Look under the port berth in the stateroom," Cole said. "There's a case left of the rum that Dad and I smuggled back from Havana last year when we were fishing a marlin tournament. How 'bout bringing a couple bottles up?"

"Aye, aye," William said, thinking how strange it was to hear someone else call his father dad.

William found the rum and climbed up the ladder holding two bottles of booze. He gave one to Cole, who was piloting the boat with their father's ashes secured on the steering console in front of him.

"Thanks," Cole said, twisting off the wax-sealed cork on his bottle.

"Cuban rum," Cole said. "Our dad said it was the best in the world. Cheers."

"Wait a minute," William said, opening his bottle. "Before we toast, how 'bout a little game of chance?"

"What do you have in mind?" Cole asked.

"First man to finish his bottle gets to keep the boat," William said.

"You're on," Cole said.

They clinked bottles and each took a huge chug. As they stopped to take a deep breath, it looked like each of them had downed about a third of his bottle. They both gulped as the rum burned going down. William tried not to cough or show any weakness, and he knew that Cole was doing the same as he put his bottle down on the console.

"How far out did you say we're going?" William asked.

"Well, it would be sixty miles if we went straight as the crow flies," Cole said, "but with the wind blowing these waves straight in our face, we'll make better time by quartering up a little to the north then sliding down some waves when we get close. I figure we've got about sixty-five miles to cover. It's gonna get a little rough on the way over, but the trip back should be like a sleigh ride."

"What's out there?" William asked.

"Treacherous waters," Cole said, "isolated as hell, strong currents, and shallow reefs. Cay Sal Bank is just a narrow spit of land. Often used as a place for drug smugglers to off-load their shit onto smaller boats from the Keys. It's also where our dad hooked up that giant blue marlin he always talked about."

It seemed to William that the booze was making his brother a little more chatty and even polite. It didn't last long.

"Those clouds out there are looking a little . . . moody, Cole," William observed.

"Moody, my ass," Cole scoffed. "Those are screamers—a real shitstorm. We can turn around if you're scared!"

"I'm not scared, Cole. I just want full disclosure. I want to know if it's a problem."

Cole picked up the bottle holding their father's ashes, looked his brother in the eye, and said, "It's not a problem, William. You're the problem. And . . . in the interest of full disclosure, this is no day to be doing this, but honestly I don't care much about anything these days and least of all you."

Saying that, he reached over and put the baling wire handle on one of the rigger clips, raised the clip to the top of the rigger, then lowered the rigger to a horizontal fishing position, thus suspending their father's ashes high over the ocean.

"What do you think you're doing with those?" William asked him.

He finished hoisting the ashes to the farthest end of the rigger and said, "Dad would have liked the view from up there."

• • •

Back on the rowboat on Loch Loon, Kyle's voice called out in excitement, interrupting the story. "Grandpa! My bobber just went down! I got a bite! I got a bite!"

"That's good," William told him. "Now keep your rod tip up."

Kyle tried to reel line in but all he got back was the sound of the screaming of his small open-face spinning reel as line flew off the spool. "Don't try to reel when he's taking line, Kyle. Let him run. Remember, fishing is like being in a prizefight. This is his round," he said, "and he'll get tired. Then you can take in some line. That'll be your round. The fight may go on and on, but be patient. The one who wins the last round, wins the fight. That's the secret to fightin' a fish, son. Got it?"

"Yeah, I think so, Grandpa. What do you think it is?" the boy asked.

Examining the bend in his fragile rod, William said, "Son, I think you've got an *Esox lucius*."

"Say what?" Kyle asked.

"A great northern pike," he answered, "a real carnivorous freshwater predator, like a barracuda in saltwater."

As the fish stopped running, Kyle reeled in some line.

"In all the time we've fished together, Grandpa, I don't think I've ever caught a big pike," the boy said. "It sure as hell is pulling."

"Hey, steady, son, watch your language. If you curse, you will not catch fish," the old man told him.

"Well, cursing sure hasn't stopped you from catchin', Gramps," he said.

"You got me there, son," the grandfather said, laughing. "Now lift up slowly and reel down. That's the way you fight fish of any size."

As Kyle cranked the reel handle, he looked over the side and said, "Grandpa! I can see him! I can see him!"

The old man looked over the side and saw the fish, too; it was indeed a pike, a beauty, maybe thirty-six inches long with a menacing jaw and green body with white dots. Occasionally it'd roll over on his back, showing its yellow-and-white belly.

Kyle was getting stronger, and the fish was tiring badly.

"Keep cranking, son," the grandfather said. "This is the last round."

William grabbed the net and scooped the exhausted fish up to the surface. He was huge and barely fit into the net. William held the fish still in the water by the side of the boat.

"I did it! I did it," Kyle shouted, grinning from ear to ear. "I caught that pike!"

"Congratulations, Kyle," he said, laughing and shaking his hand. "Now it's in your blood. You're ruined for life."

"Grandpa?" Kyle asked. "Do we keep him or let him go?"

"Kyle, that's up to you," he told him. "It's your fish. We can let him go or we can keep him and have our chef at the restaurant cook him for dinner."

Looking troubled, Kyle said, "Do I have to choose?"

"Yes, you do. That's what we grown-ups have to do every day," William said. "We make choices in our lives, and it's not always easy. But you're lucky today because there's no wrong answer here, buddy. There are a lot of pike in this lake, and they make great eating—you wouldn't be wasting it. Or, if you like, we can release him. There is honor either way."

Kyle paused to think, then said, "I want to release him," making his old granddad smile.

"Okay then," William said. "Lean over here and watch how I do this. Pike are toothy critters and can take off a finger if you're not careful."

William took out a pair of needle-nose pliers and carefully removed the hook from the fish's lip. Then he opened the net in the water—and with a thrust of his big tail, the pike was gone in a flash.

"Wow," Kyle said, "that was great. Thanks, Grandpa. Now I want to catch one for dinner."

"Let's do it, buddy," he said.

They baited their hooks and began fishing again. Kyle leaned back on his flotation cushion and said, "So, you're heading to sea with Cole and there's a storm coming."

"Yeah," William said, "there was a storm coming outside the boat and inside it as well."

• • •

By now, William and Cole were pretty well into the afternoon and still running toward their destination. The late-day sun broke in and out of some ominous-looking towering stratus clouds. The wind was picking up and the swells were increasing. Then Cole pulled back on the throttle, bringing them to trolling speed. He put on the autopilot to keep the boat on the correct compass course.

Cole put down the other outrigger and said, "C'mon down," as he climbed down the ladder. When he got to the cockpit he set out two trolling lines.

"What are we doing?" William asked him.

"We're fishin'," Cole said. "Lotta critters out here. Might as well try and catch some nice mahi mahi for dinner. We can grill it up with some lime juice."

"So how far are we from Cay Sal Bank?" William asked.

Cole just gazed out at the angry ocean with its waves swelling up in all directions. He seemed to look up at the dark-purple clouds as they twisted and towered. He raised both arms to the raging sea and shouted, "We're there!"

Then he examined his rum bottle next to William's to see that he led the challenge by about an inch. Taking a deep breath, he chugged the rest of his rum, held his empty bottle up, and said, "It looks like the boat's mine."

"Congratulations," William said. "You deserve it."

Laughing, Cole ran another baited hook up one of the riggers and set the butt end of the rod down in a rod holder.

"He knew he was dying, didn't he?" William asked Cole.

"Heart attack, man. There's no way of tellin'," Cole said.

"Why'd he call me then?" William asked. "Why after all this time, after all these years? Why did he call me that night?"

Cole paused, looked him in the eye, and said, "The tailor."

"The what?" William said.

"He always kept tabs on you through the tailor."

"Through Bernard?"

"Yeah, the old Scotsman, as Dad would say. He called that night and told Dad about your public meltdown. Dad figured you'd need to get out of New York and lay low for a while."

William was stunned. "And you went along with it, the whole deal?"

"I had no say in the matter, did I? Anyway, it wasn't for you, dummy," Cole shouted. "It was important to him."

William felt his anger growing and shouted, "Important to him? Oh really? Do you know that when my mother was on her deathbed dying of dementia eleven years ago, he left her? Didn't even have the decency to come to her funeral . . . to honor her, because he was on some fucking fishing trip to Panama and the black marlin were running. You and your mother, the mighty Mrs. Reno, were probably with him for all I know."

"Mrs. Reno, my what?" Cole yelled at him.

"Your mother," William shouted back. "I saw all those pictures of the three of you in her office . . ."

"William," Cole yelled, "you are truly an ignorant asshole. Mrs. Reno is not my mother. My mother was a dancer in town at a joint named Woody's. I was an angry problem child. A bastard with no father. I was skipping school and getting into trouble all the time. One day when I was fifteen, two buddies of mine and I stole a car, went for a joyride, and got arrested. My mother had enough. She left, just left. Went up north with a trucker. I haven't heard a word from her since.

"There I was stuck in jail and Mrs. Reno got me out and offered me free room and board if I would clean up her restaurant every night. I never even met Leo, our father, till I was twenty-one."

Cole was wound up now and yelled, "While you were growin' up in the lap of luxury with your rich mommy and daddy, I was a bastard kid scrubbing urinals, washing toilets and cleaning up drunks' puke in a gin mill to get by. Now I have you crying up a river and you know what I say? I say fuck you and your dead mother!"

The rage was back, and William knew it was time. He stormed to the salon and grabbed the rosewood box, brought it out to the cockpit, opened it up, and tossed one of the pistols to Cole.

Thunder rolled in the distance as flecks of rain began to fall around the two brothers. Cole looked amazed.

William stepped back, cocked his pistol, and pointed it right between Cole's eyes. Cole looked at William at first in disbelief; then he slowly cocked and raised his pistol as well till William was looking right down its barrel. Through his anger and hatred, and despite everything, William respected this man's courage.

"Say that again, Cole, I fuckin' dare you to say it again," William shouted.

By now the storm was raging and the two brothers were standing in the cockpit of the old fishing boat staring each other down over the sights of their cocked pistols.

"When did she die?" Cole shouted over the storm.

"What?" William yelled back.

"Your mom, when did she die?"

"Christmas Day, ten years ago."

Strangely, Cole lowered his pistol, and his look of rage turned into a look of sadness.

"He wasn't fishing," Cole said.

"What do you mean?"

"When your mom died, our father was in Panama but he wasn't fishing," Cole said.

"Well, what was he doing then?" William asked, still pointing his pistol at Cole's head.

"He was bailing my ass out of Panamanian prison," Cole said. "I was looking at life for trafficking. They allowed me one call. The only person I could think of to call was Mrs. Reno, who called our dad. He brought a bunch of money and came down there for me. It nearly busted him, but he got me out."

William was speechless. He took his finger off the trigger and relaxed his gun.

Cole added, "And I had no idea about your mother. I'm sorry.

"I knew how proud he was of you," Cole went on. "Sometimes on the boat that's all he'd talk about. It made me feel useless."

Now it was Cole's turn to soften. "I also know that he felt he'd burned his bridges up north and was embarrassed about how he left . . . and now I know why."

William's rage had vanished and he found himself looking at Cole for the first time as his brother.

Then looking at the bottle of ashes William said, "I would imagine that if I were him, I'd have done the same thing."

Cole nodded. With that, William knew exactly what to do. With a quick sweep of his arm, he swung the pistol up and took careful aim at the bottle hanging from the rigger. The gun fired and the bottle full of ashes exploded. The ashes seemed to hang in the air as if in slow motion before they swirled in the wind and disappeared into the waves of the raging ocean.

William looked at the pistol and then threw it into the ocean as far as he could. Cole laughed and did the same with his.

All of a sudden there was a huge flash of lightning and roar of thunder as one of the trolling lines that Cole had rigged started flying off the reel, which made an angry hissing noise. The rod bent over double.

Cole looked at his brother and mouthed the understatement of the day: *Big fish.*

"How big?" William asked.

"Marlin big," he said, then added, "How much were those dueling pistols worth?"

"I don't know," William said, "fifteen or twenty thousand, maybe. Why?"

"I think we overpaid the fish!" Cole laughed. "You ready for this?"

"Hell yes!" William shouted.

Cole grabbed a wide, brown leather fighting belt from a cupboard. As he finished cinching it around William's waist, the monster fish flashed up from the depths and shot fully out of the water, twisting and somersaulting.

"Oh my God," Cole yelled. "She's friggin' huge, must weigh fifteen or sixteen hundred pounds!"

"Dad's marlin?" William asked.

"Might well be," Cole said, "just might well be.

"All right," he told William, "when I tell you, loosen the drag on the reel a little by pulling this lever back half an inch so you can lift the rod out of the rod holder and put the butt of the rod in your fighting belt."

"Wait a minute, you're the expert," William said.

"That's right, and I'm also the captain and I gotta run the boat."

"Well, don't you have one of those nice big fighting chairs?" William asked.

Cole said, laughing, "No, not on this boat. We fight fish the same way we piss, like men—standing up!"

With that he climbed up the ladder, turned off the autopilot, and nudged the throttle forward a little. "You ready?" he shouted from the bridge.

"No, wait a minute," William said, taking a huge swig and finishing the rum in his bottle. Then he yelled, "Ready."

"Do it!" the captain ordered.

William loosened the drag and grabbed the rod and felt the fish's weight as he lifted it from the rod holder. It was a major struggle to get the butt section into the rod belt. No doubt feeling the drag pressure change, the big marlin came out of the water and took off at full speed away from the boat.

The power of the marlin's surge pulled William to the very back of the cockpit. Jamming his knees into the transom, he held on for dear life.

Cole, seeing his situation, calmly yelled down from the bridge, "Hey, big brother, you better loosen that drag a little unless you really want to swim with the fishes this afternoon."

William did as he was told and bought himself a short breather. As it would turn out, they had bigger problems than that fish. While they fought on, the winds seemed to increase to gale force and the heavens opened up on them. As chains of lightning ripped across the sky, with thunder crashing all around them, they were pelted with a driving rain that felt like hail, and it was. Hailstones, some the size of golf balls, bounced off the deck. Then William's rod started buzzing with static electricity. He knew that was not good. He was basically standing in a storm holding a long lightning rod. *Damn the torpedoes*, he thought. He wanted to catch this monster, and there was nowhere to hide anyway.

Just then he heard Cole yell, "Watch out," and looked up in time to see a fifteen-foot wave building to hit them broadside. The concussion of the wave knocked William to his knees as he struggled to hold on to the rod. He got back to his feet just to see the ankle-deep water on the deck rushing down into the engine room.

All of a sudden the running lights went out, followed promptly by the engine going dead. Then there was darkness, rain and the howling winds punctuated by flashes of lightning and deafening explosions of thunder.

William fought to keep his balance in the cockpit and to keep his line tight on the marlin. On the bridge Cole struggled to restart the engine and keep the boat under some control.

"What's going on, Cole?" William yelled.

"We've lost our electronics," Cole yelled back.

"That sounds bad."

"It ain't good."

With no forward motion the *Keys Disease* pitched and yawed dangerously in the dark waves.

"Whatever happens," Cole yelled to him, "you hold on to that fish. Don't let her go."

William watched Cole grab a battery-powered waterproof spotlight and shine it first on the cockpit and then into the waves.

"There's a reef around here somewhere," Cole yelled. "I can't find the goddamn reef!"

Suddenly, there was a horrific crunching sound and William thought, *I think the reef just found us*. Once again they were taking on water. William figured that the jagged coral of the reef had stoved in their hull. Still he held on to the rod.

William heard Cole yelling into a radio, "Mayday, Mayday, *Keys Disease* calling, Mayday."

Just then the boat lurched almost onto its side as another wave battered it into the reef. William looked up to see his brother lose his balance on the wet and slippery bridge, then lose his footing and tumble off the bridge ten feet to crash hard on the floor of the cockpit next to where William was trying to keep standing.

"Cole, Cole," William yelled to his brother, who was lying facedown on the deck. Lightning crashed again and illuminated the sky as their monster marlin jumped into the electrical air not fifty feet away from them.

William looked at the fish, then at his brother lying crippled on the deck, and then at the rod in his hand. He shouted to the wind, "Okay, old man, you can have him. He's all yours. Tight lines and rest in peace." With that, he threw the rod, still hooked to the marlin, over the side and scrambled to his brother.

"Cole! Cole, can you hear me?" William shouted. Nothing.

The boat was lying sideways against the reef, and every wave that hit them was accompanied by a cracking sound of something else breaking.

William put his arms around Cole, pulled his head up out of the water on the deck, and sat him up against the tackle station built into the boat's bulkhead.

Eventually, Cole grunted in pain, and his eyes opened slowly.

"Cole!"

"What happened to the marlin?" Cole asked.

"Broke off when we hit the reef," William lied.

"Shit."

"Can you move?" William asked.

"Don't think so," Cole said. "I think some of my ribs are broke."

"We need life jackets," William said.

"They're in the salon under the seats," Cole said.

William forced the salon door open, found two life jackets, and brought them back, carefully fitting one on Cole and putting the other on himself.

"Could this boat sink?" William asked him.

"Yeah, we're wedged against the reef and eventually these waves will cause the hull to tear apart. There's a life raft down below."

"Okay, I can get it," William said.

"No, that's my job," Cole said. "I know where it is. I'll get it. You need to get up to the bridge and find a small portable transponder unit with a battery backup.

It's in a yellow waterproof case under the pilot's console. There's a flare gun in the case as well."

The boat rocked wildly. "You gonna be all right?" William asked him.

"Yeah, just get that yellow transponder case and get back down here as fast as you can.

"And William . . ." he said as his brother turned to look at him.

"Yeah," William said.

"Watch your ass, man. I don't want you dyin' before I get the chance to kill you."

William laughed. "Likewise, Cole," he said. "After all, you're the only family I've got left."

They both smiled.

The boat was now lying at a dangerous angle as the waves battered it against the reef. William tied the handheld spotlight to the fighting belt that he was still wearing, reached out and gripped the ladder, and with white knuckles slowly made his way, rung over rung, to the bridge. Lightning flashed all around.

William crawled on his hands and knees to the console and dug through the equipment hatch until he found the transponder in the yellow waterproof oil-skin satchel. He threw it over his shoulder just as there came the horrible crunching sound of the boat's hull buckling.

The water flooding the hull changed the sportfish's balance and the boat rolled over on its side. William took a deep breath and dove from the bridge as another giant wave rose and crashed over the capsized boat.

William hit the foaming, black turbulent water hard, then flailed his arms and kicked his feet, struggling to reach the air. Finally, aided by his life vest, he popped to the surface gasping. William wiped his eyes and blinked to see that the *Keys Disease* had rolled all the way over and was now lying upside down against the reef. He tried to dive down to look into the salon window but his life vest was holding him up, making it impossible. He slipped off the flotation device and with the transponder still around his shoulder, grabbed the spotlight, turned it on, took the biggest breath he could, and dove to the window. In the beam of the spotlight he could see the closed salon filling with water, but there was no sign of Cole.

William resurfaced and swam around to the stern of the boat and dove again to the salon door, then, pulling hard, tried to slide open one of the sliding pocket doors. He couldn't budge it. He shone the light in the window and from this angle saw his brother inside struggling to keep his head above the water and into the top bit of space to breathe in what looked to be about a foot of air trapped in a pocket there. He knew that air pocket wasn't going to last long, as the water in the salon was rising fast.

Frantically now, William kicked to the surface to find something to use to smash the door in. All of a sudden some piece of debris hit him in the back of the head—it was the rosewood pistol case. He grabbed it and dove down again to the salon window. Holding the wooden case, he jammed it as hard as he could against the glass then held up the spotlight to see that he had cracked the window. Three more smashes of the box and the window shattered. Aided by the rush of water from the outside, he was able to kick in all of the glass before swimming into the cabin. William surfaced face-to-face with his brother, gasping for air in the small air pocket that remained.

"Forget it," Cole said, "you can have the boat."

"What about the raft?" William asked him.

"I already got it," Cole said. "Let's get out of here!"

Cole and William made their way to the window, pushed out the raft, then pulled their way out of the salon.

Reaching the surface the brothers kicked their way through the broiling sea. Waves crashed down on them, threatening to wrest the life raft out of their grasp, but they both held on to it as if fighting for their very lives.

When they got to a safe distance from the reef and what remained of the boat, they undid the snaps that kept the raft folded and Cole pulled the cord that released the CO_2. They held their breath, then even over the storm heard the rush of air as the circumference of the little craft popped into shape.

William pulled himself into the raft then helped Cole climb in as well. He noticed that there were a couple of paddles inside.

It was obvious that Cole was in a lot of pain.

"How are your ribs?" William said.

"Not so good," Cole said, "and I think I may have broken my leg, too."

Cole also had a nasty gash on his shin that was bleeding profusely. *Not a good thing*, William thought, *in shark-filled waters*.

"Must have happened when the boat turned over," Cole said.

"Well, we can cut up my shirt for a tourniquet and use those paddles and my fighting belt for a splint," William said, "but it's gonna hurt."

"Go for it, Will. Just cinch it tight and let's get it over with."

William went about creating the splint: laying out the belt, cutting it in half with the knife from Cole's belt, and preparing the makeshift device.

"You ready, Cole?" he said.

Cole put his hand on William's shoulder and said, "Just do it, bro."

William pulled the first strap tight around his brother's leg and the paddles. Cole yelled out in pain and then passed out. William tightened the second strap, took off his shirt, and fashioned it into a tourniquet to try to stop the bleeding.

With Cole out for the count, William performed a close inspection of the raft. There didn't seem to be any air leaks, and they were not taking on any water. Then he checked to be sure that the transponder was working. That done, he sat back for what he hoped wouldn't be too long a vigil.

He reflected on everything that had happened in his life during the past week. Lightning continued to flash in the sky and thunder seemed to engulf the little raft. Almost instinctively, William said a prayer for his father's soul and asked that he and his brother survive this storm so that they might get to know each other. Then as the storm raged around them, totally exhausted, he fell asleep.

CHAPTER 19

THE RESCUE

Next thing William knew he was waking up to the first light of dawn. The storm had moved through; he could see lightning way off in the distance. The bright stars of Gemini appeared between the drifting clouds in the sky. The churning sea had been replaced by huge dark swells, well spaced and regular, offering no imminent danger to their little raft.

He looked over at Cole, who was still out. His breathing was regular although occasionally he moaned softly. William put his hand on his brother's forehead; it felt cool, as if he didn't have a fever. Gently putting his thumb and two fingers on Cole's wrist, he checked his brother's pulse and heartbeat: regular. Then he examined the splint and the tourniquet, which seemed to be holding up fine. The gash on Cole's shin looked ugly but it had stopped bleeding.

William sat back to wait, watching their transponder blinking silently. He looked out at the sea rising and falling around their raft and was suddenly shocked to see about six large black fins heading toward them. *Sharks.*

He felt it was time to wake up his brother for this. He said, "Cole, Cole wake up!" Cole didn't respond. He put his hand on Cole's shoulder and shook him. "Cole, please wake up."

Cole opened his eyes slowly, then grimaced as he felt his pain. "What?" he said.

All William could do was point toward the approaching fins. Cole raised his head, took a look, and then put his head back down. "What's the matter," he said, "you afraid of a few bottlenose dolphins?"

Greatly relieved, William sat back to watch the approaching pod. Four large gray adults and their young, two small calves, greyhounding through the water toward the brothers and at the last minute diving under their raft, being careful not to hit or endanger them. Then almost as one, they turned, repeated the maneuver, and swam randomly around the raft as if they were saying hello, or checking up on them, or merely wanted to play.

William turned to his brother.

"How're you feelin', Cole?"

"I've felt better," he said, "but I'll make it. Thanks for all you did."

"Just tried to think of what you would have done," William said, "if you hadn't killed me, that is."

Cole flinched when he laughed and said, "That hurt my ribs, no more jokes."

"So Cole," William asked, "do you think we'll get rescued soon?"

"Yeah sure, man," Cole answered. "You're such a big shot and now a media darling, I'm sure that the New

York press has put out an all-points alert and launched a full-scale search. They probably want to know if you've shot anyone with those pistols of yours . . . like an indigent Keys fishing guide."

"Great!" William answered. "How 'bout you playing dead then to help build up my image?"

"Sure, whatever I can do to help," Cole said. "Seriously, with that transponder beepin', I'm sure that someone's tracking us and will scramble to come get us now that the storm's over."

"That's good," William said, "but I sure wish I had that mobile phone that you tossed in the drink."

"Yeah, that was pretty good," Cole said. "I guess that I hated you for so long, I was really trying hard to bait you into a fight so I could kick the shit out of you."

"And now?" William asked.

Cole said, "Now we're on the same team. I feel like you were with our father for his first life, and I was with him for his second, but I'm glad that we both had the chance to be with him in the end."

This statement hung between them as they swayed in the raft. In a while, Cole said, "By the way, I guess I didn't help you much with that Jenny Hunter, did I?"

"No problem," William said. "I'm afraid that that was a self-inflicted wound, just like the one on my forehead."

"You know it's bleeding again, don't you?" Cole said.

"Yeah, I figured so. Guess I'd better have someone look at it when we get in."

The life raft drifted for a while as the morning sun beat down on the brothers. William broke the silence with a short laugh.

"What?" Cole asked him.

"Well, I was just thinking," William said, "you're my brother and for all the time we've been together these past few days and everything we've been through, I don't even know your last name. Is it McKay?"

"No," Cole said. "It's Snow. My mother chose it . . . it's the street name for cocaine. She thought it was a big joke. I wasn't much amused, so I decided just to go by my first name."

"Yeah," William said, "some joke all right. So tell me, Cole, what's the first thing you're gonna do when you get home?"

Cole looked his brother in the eye and said without hesitation, "Go fishin', of course. It's what I do. It's who I am. How 'bout you, Will?"

"Well," William said after a long pause, "I think I need to do some work on discovering who I am so I can find my life. I'm going to start, though, by releasing four sharks who I've shared an office with. I think they'll like getting out of New York and reintroduced to the ocean. That'll be a first step toward finding my own happiness. What do you think?"

Cole didn't answer. William looked over to see that his brother had closed his eyes and fallen back to sleep.

After about an hour, far off in the distance, there came a sound . . . a sound that William recognized from a long time ago . . . a helicopter. Cole opened his eyes, while William dug through their transponder bag to find the flare gun, raised it, and fired it into the morning sky.

A large long-range Bahamian coast guard helicopter soared in toward them, causing the water to rush around them and into the raft. Seeing Cole's condition, the crew lowered a rescue litter basket, and William helped Cole into it. As they hoisted Cole out of the raft, William flashed back to some similar experiences he'd had with the helicopter evacuations of injured troops from the jungles and rice fields of Vietnam. Some of those results hadn't been very good, so he forced those thoughts out of his mind.

With Cole secured, it was William's turn. The rescuers lowered a yoke to him. He put it over his head and under his arms, gave 'em a thumbs-up sign, and up he went. Once on board, William saw that the medical crew had already hooked up an IV to Cole's arm and were giving him a shot and attending to his injured leg. Cole looked at him and smiled as they hooked William up to an IV as well and handed him a plastic bottle of ice water.

As William enjoyed a long drink, a crewman looked over at him and said, "You are lucky, mon!"

"Yeah, tell me about it," William said.

"No, no, no, mon," the crewman said, "not because of de accident and de rescue . . . at de new hospital, we've got a brand-new lady doctor! Her name is Hunter, but she's so fine, we call her de fox. She'll take good care of you, mon."

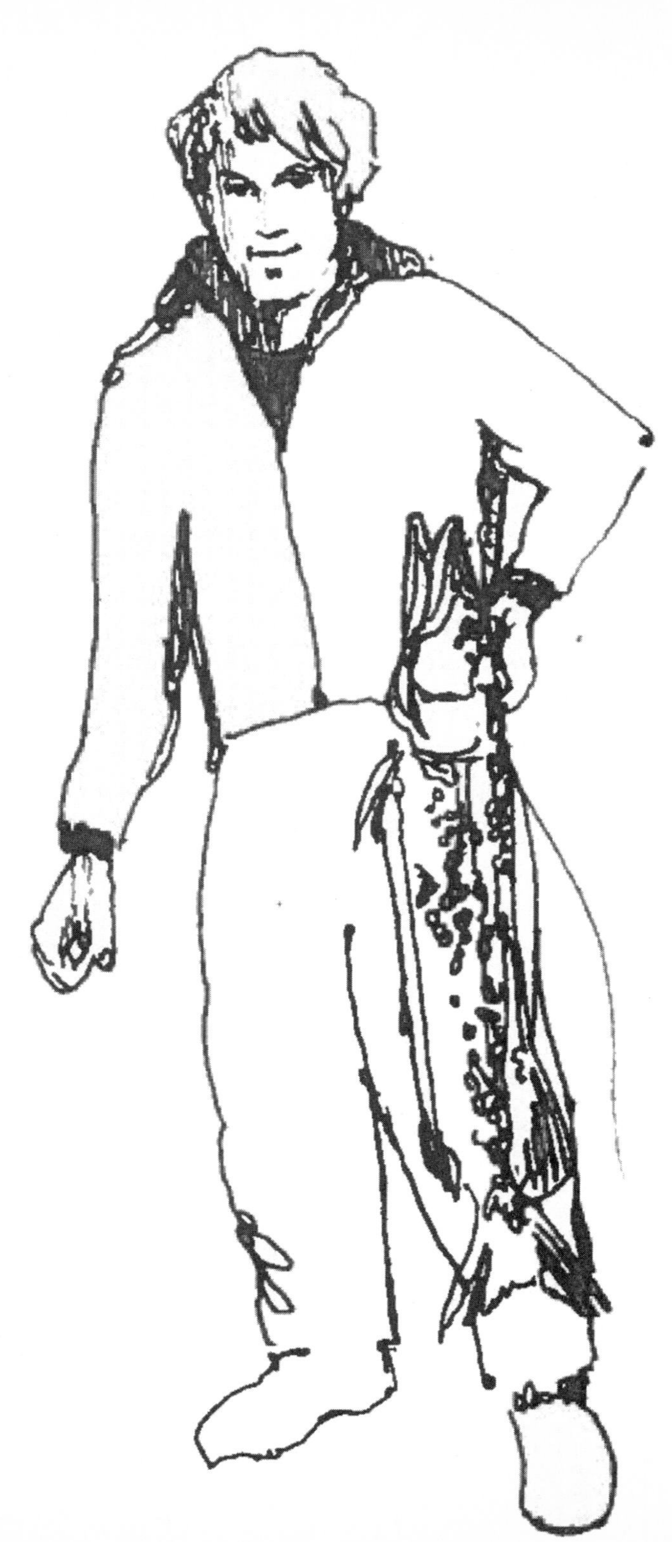

CHAPTER 20

THE FISHING DAY ENDS

As William and his grandson, Kyle, rowed toward the mooring dock of the Turtle restaurant, Kyle said, "Whatever happened to your brother, Grandpa?"

"Well, son," William said, "we stayed at the clinic in Bimini for about three days until he was strong enough to travel and then returned to Islamorada. After our adventure, I offered Cole a job and some stock in my company, but in typical Cole fashion, he declined. I believe his exact words were, 'And be miserable like you? What the hell would I want to do a dumb-ass thing like that for?'"

• • •

Finally back in Islamorada, William gathered up his stuff and got ready to head for the airport in Marathon. Cole demanded to drive him down there in their dad's old truck, broken leg and all. Cole was one tough cookie, William thought, as he helped Dorado clamber into the bed of the truck for the ride then climbed into the passenger seat.

When they got to Marathon Jet Center and pulled up to the G2, Captain Harding was waiting and even threw William a salute.

"Hand me my crutches from the back, will you, Will?" Cole said. "I want to get a view of this bird close up."

Cole climbed out of the truck and the brothers stood together by the plane. "Last chance, Cole," William said. "You want to reconsider my offer and fly with me to New York?"

Without hesitation Cole said to William, "When pigs fly out my ass!"

William laughed and put out his hand to him, then, instinctively, he dropped his hand and gave his brother a big hug. Cole hugged him back, his crutches falling to the tarmac. William looked him in the eye and said, "Cole, I'm glad to have you as my brother."

Cole said, "You too, bro."

William bent over and picked up the crutches and handed them to his brother, happy that his new sunglasses hid the tears welling in his eyes.

"Tight lines," William said and walked up the stairs into the plane.

The plane taxied down the runway, turned, and took off. William looked out the window to see Cole still standing by the truck and waving good-bye.

Cole and William had vowed to stay close and take a fishing trip together every Christmas. In fact, they vowed a lot of things but both got busy and it never happened. They talked a few times on the phone but that was the last time they ever saw each other. One day, a few years later, William got a call from Mrs. Reno. Cole had been flying over the Gulf of Mexico with a friend spotting tarpon and apparently flew too slow, causing the plane to stall. It crashed headfirst into the ocean.

"I'm so sorry," Mrs. Reno had said to William. "Cole had a picture that he wanted you to have if anything ever happened to him. I just mailed it to you. Let me know when it arrives."

• • •

The grandfather and grandson slowed their boat as it reached the mooring.

"So, Kyle," William said to his grandson, after clearing his throat and taking a deep breath, "Cole is more like a legend to me now, a ghost brother to fish with, a constant reminder to me to truly live each day of my life and to always say the things that need to be said when we still have the chance to say them.

"Life is tough, Kyle, and none of us gets a free pass. Part of growing up is learning that regardless of age or circumstance, everyone is trying to figure it out and get by. Parents are no exception. They're not perfect. Keep an open mind and an open heart. It gets bad sometimes, but things will work out. I promise you."

The little boat pulled up to the dock and the grandfather congratulated his grandson on the two pike he'd caught, the second of which lay in the bottom of the boat covered with melting ice from the cooler and an old green towel.

The old man could hear music coming from the bar of the Turtle. The boy gave the old man a smile and said, "So, Grandpa, how much of that story should I believe?"

The old man smiled, too, and said, "As much as you dare, my boy," and extended his hand. "But remember our deal. You keep this one between us, okay?"

"Okay," the boy said, giving his grandpa a big hug.

"Now go give your catch to the chef," William said.

With the pike on a thin rope, the boy jumped up on the dock and began walking toward the restaurant, then paused and looked back at the old man.

"Grandpa?" he asked. "Do you ever wish you hadn't let the marlin go?"

William thought and said, "I let more go than a fish that day, buddy, a lot more, and I never regretted it for a moment."

Smiling, the boy said, "Can we go fishing again tomorrow, Grandpa?"

"I think we can work something out," William answered, watching his grandson proudly bound up the stairs to the Turtle.

The man slowly climbed out of the little rowboat, stretched for a minute, and tied his lines to two dock posts. What had he really let go that day in the storm?

He'd let go of the anger he'd felt all those years over his father walking out on him. It had taken a long time, but he'd finally come to realize what he'd just shared with his own grandson. Parents aren't as perfect as they would like appear to their children. They are from a different generation, but human, dealing as best they know how with their own sets of problems.

He'd let go of hatred for a sibling—a brother he hadn't even known he had. He'd walked in that younger man's shoes, been a part of his life for a short while, and seen the demons that he'd had to confront.

And finally, he'd let go of the smoldering rage that had all but consumed him. He'd realized that loneliness can be a function of loss of faith in those closest to us. And by letting go of the rage, he'd opened his heart to the opportunity to discover love.

As he opened the door of the Turtle, the sound of live music embraced him. He paused to listen to a very familiar song, "Unforgettable," and smiled.

"Yes, my life has been good," William said to himself. "I have no complaints. I'm a happy man, and after all, I got the girl and found true love."

He took off his sunglasses and looked in to see his wife, Jenny, still beautiful in her sixties, singing into the microphone to a cheering crowd.

Jenny's eyes lit up and she waved to her husband as he walked in.

Over in a corner, William saw his grandson, Kyle, standing with his mom examining an old framed photograph on the restaurant wall. William knew that the old photograph was of three men standing by an old truck in a Florida marina. One was an old angler, the second a swarthy fishing guide, and the third a peculiar fellow with a cut on his forehead in a filthy tuxedo.

ACKNOWLEDGMENTS

Overriding thanks to Zachary "Zach" Dean, a thoughtful and talented screenplay writer/teacher whose creative collaboration gave me so much more than an outline for this, my first novel. I hope that his forthcoming movie, *Guide*, becomes a box office smash.

My friend John "Swany" Swan, a wonderful naturalist artist from Maine painted the cover, which I believe captures the important interaction between generations in an outdoor setting.

Craig "Bula" Reagor used pen and ink to draw the chapter openers, helping the characters and action to come to life.

Craig also joined Judy "the Good Witch" Roth, Sandy "Sid" Moret and his wife, Sue, to read and candidly critique my manuscript, for which I am grateful. My assistant, Kate Hart, never once frowned about my rewrites.

Thanks to Luke "Meat" Dempsey, an accomplished Brit ex-pat writer/editor, for teaching me how not to waste words and Fred Bimbler, who has represented me for six years.

I also appreciate the efforts of my friend of ten years, Meryl Moss, and am also indebted to my friends Pete Johnson and Kevin Aman.

It's great to be back with Tony Lyons and Jay Cassell at Skyhorse. So much has happened since they published my first book in 2001.

It was also a pleasure working with their editor, Nicole Frail.

And finally, I want to thank my wife, Mindy, who continues to use her enormous skills as a producer to help me create a life worth living and some books that are, hopefully, worth reading.